TURN OF
FORTUNE

TURN OF FORTUNE

•

Vicky Hunnings

AVALON BOOKS
NEW YORK

MYS   OS-333   # 23580

For Brad, a wonderful son and good friend.
No mother could ask for more.

I would like to thank my father, Robert Rouse, and son, Brad Hunnings, for their continued support. And I could not have written this book without the help of my sister, Debra Rouse. Not only does she let me bounce ideas off her at all hours of the day and night, she helps edit my manuscripts draft after draft. She also shows this computer-challenged writer all the amazing things a PC can do.

Donnie and Julie Gillett were kind enough to share their experiences in Belize, along with their photos and several tour books, which was helpful.

Special thanks to the members of my writing critique group: Kathy Wall and Jo Williams. Both are talented writers with a lot of patience. If you haven't read their books, you should.

I'd like to thank Harry Skevington for creating and maintaining my website. He and his wife Pat have been steadfast and treasured friends for many years.

Thanks to my editor, Erin Cartwright-Niumata, who always makes good suggestions to improve my manuscripts.

And, to Grace and Ryan, thanks for letting Grandma come and play when she needs a break from writing.

Chapter One

The slender, middle-aged man rested the barrel of the AR15 rifle on the windowsill. He stared down from the top floor of the deserted warehouse to the crowded street below. His mark should be along shortly. He'd been shadowing her for days, and she usually took this route on her way home from art class.

He wiped the sweat from his brow on the arm of his black T-shirt. He was eager to finish this job and get out of the city. August in Paris was not a fun place to be, especially for someone who preferred the coolness of the mountains.

He wondered about the woman. What had she done? What knowledge did she possess that required her to be silenced? She was attractive—many would say beautiful—and young, probably in her late twenties.

He changed positions, his knees and back aching. He was getting too old for this. And he didn't like to do women. He'd killed two in the past, but only because they had infiltrated his IRA unit and deserved it.

He bit into an apple from his knapsack and tried to relax his stiff muscles for a moment. She probably wouldn't be along for another five minutes or so. Did she have any idea that she had only a few more minutes to live? Nothing in her manner as he'd watched her these last several days indicated she was aware of any type of threat. That she had seen her last sunrise, eaten her last meal, and would never make love

1

again. As always, these thoughts gave him a feeling of power.

Spotting his prey about a block away, he set his apple aside and took his position.

Marissa Langford was enjoying the sunny day, her mind on the sketches she'd made in class. She darted between cars lined up in the stalled traffic along the Rue Victor Hugo.

"Excuse me. Could I bother you for the time?" a heavyset man on her left asked. The sun in her eyes, Marissa turned away from the glare and bent her head to look down at her watch.

"It's one-twenty," she said as she felt the man lunge into her, sending both of them sprawling to the pavement. Glancing curiously, people stepped around them and hurried on their way.

Marissa extricated herself, reached over, and gently shook the man. "Are you okay?"

There was no response. Fearful he might have had a stroke or heart attack, Marissa shook him again. Still, he did not react.

"Is there a problem?" A young man in a three-piece, pin-striped suit knelt down beside them.

Marissa glanced at his handsome face, thankful for the compassion in his expression and the concern in his eyes and voice. "He just collapsed. I'm afraid he may have had a heart attack or something. Can you help me roll him over on his back?"

"Sure," he said, placing his briefcase down on the pavement. "Let's do it on the count of three."

They struggled with the prone man's weight. As soon as they turned him, Marissa gasped. Blood stained the front of his shirt and there was a small puddle on the sidewalk. His face had two ugly abrasions from the fall. The Good Samaritan leaned down, his face close to the man's nose.

"He's not breathing. It looks like he's been shot."

"Shot?"

"Yes, look at that hole in his shirt."

A female pedestrian saw the blood and screamed, "Someone call an ambulance!"

Suddenly a crowd formed around them. The young man placed his fingers over the victim's carotid artery, checking for a pulse. He found none. "I don't think we need to try CPR. He's already dead."

Marissa could hear sirens a short distance away. She stared at the blood on her hands. She was momentarily transported back to another time, another place, where someone else's blood had stained her hands.

"Sorry, but I've got to go." She jumped up and darted into the crowd.

"Wait!" the man called after her. "The police will want to talk to you."

As Marissa slipped away, she fought the urge to run, trying instead to blend in with the other pedestrians. She wouldn't let herself think about what had just happened until she'd made her way back to her apartment and bolted the door behind her.

She raced to the sink and washed the blood off her hands. Marissa realized she was shaking uncontrollably. She filled the teapot with water, placed it on the stove, and leaned against the counter, her mind racing.

It was the second time she'd been standing next to someone who'd been shot. Her mind flashed back to the first, when her bridegroom, Marcus DeSilva, was murdered on the steps of the church on their wedding day in Hilton Head, South Carolina, almost two years ago.

At least this time she hadn't known the man or been a suspect in his death. Were the gendarmes looking for her? Why had she run away and not waited to talk to them?

The teapot whistled. She removed it from the stove, poured some water into her mug, and pulled an Earl Grey tea bag out of the canister.

She sat down at the table. She knew why she'd run. She'd had her fill of cops after her husband's death, not an experience she cared to repeat: the constant questions over and over, delving into her checkered past, feeling as if, any minute, she was about to be arrested.

As she sipped the tea, she wondered who the dead man was and why he'd been shot. A jealous spouse, an irate investor, a thief?

Marissa replayed the scene over and over in her mind. Should she contact the police? Did she know anything that might help them? If she hadn't turned to get the sun out of her eyes, she might have seen more.

Then a chill crept down her spine. She sat frozen— stunned by the new thought that had just occurred to her.

Were her sins coming back to haunt her?

Chapter Two

Andrea Michaels knew she was dying as she watched the poison slide slowly from the IV tube into her arm. Drip, drip, drip. Sixty-two drops per minute.

She counted the ceiling tiles again. The number hadn't changed since the last time she'd been in this room just a month before. She always hated this part, the waiting. She couldn't even read since her left arm was taped to an armboard, so she slipped on the earphones to her CD player and tried to relax as the sound of the ocean and the cry of a loon carried her back in time . . .

Just eighteen months before, Andrea had thought she finally had her life on track. She'd started a medical transcription business, had struggled at first, but had built her client list to the point where she was toying with the idea of hiring someone to help her. She'd just met Michael Bateman, who turned her ordinary world upside down as fast as a three hundred and sixty-degree roller coaster. By the second date, she was envisioning a fairytale wedding. It wasn't long before she was spending more time at his place than at her own.

Two months later, she noticed a little vaginal spotting. She'd made an appointment with her gynecologist and been shocked when he informed her she was pregnant. Not only was she on the pill, but she'd insisted Michael use a condom as well. After a few days, she'd gotten over her initial shock and had been pleased about the pregnancy. But her joy was short-lived when a sonogram could find no evidence of a fetus.

After multiple blood tests and believing she might have a rare form of cancer, her doctor insisted she have an immediate hysterectomy. All her childhood dreams of some day being a mother had vanished as quickly as oxygen in a smoke-filled room.

Following the surgery, the doctors all agreed she should undergo a round of chemotherapy since her blood test remained elevated for the hormone human chorionic gonatropin, in spite of the fact that her pathology report had shown no evidence of uterine cancer.

For the next three months, she'd suffered through all the expected side effects from the deadly drugs, including the loss of her hair. The memory of toweling her hair dry after a shower and finding clumps of her golden curls almost made her nauseated.

After she'd completed the chemotherapy, she slowly began to get her strength back and regain some of the thirty pounds she'd lost. Later, she'd placed her wig on the top shelf of the closet and tried to get used to her short, spiky style.

But the blood tests remained elevated, and the doctors believed her cancer continued unchecked. They were frustrated they couldn't identify the primary site.

At that point, Michael had told her he just wasn't man enough to handle the situation . . .

Andrea heard the nurse enter her room but didn't open her eyes. She couldn't stand the pity she always saw reflected on the faces of the staff. She doubted they had many twenty-seven-year-olds dying from cancer.

Ivy Hansen had been working with patients trying to fight the big C for almost twenty years. She'd seen a lot of people pass through, but this one was so young. She checked the IV, then glanced at Andrea. She appeared to be asleep or lost in meditation. She felt sorry for the young girl. She'd just read her history. This was her second round of chemotherapy. A few weeks ago they'd found some shadows on her spleen and rushed her off to surgery again, only to find no evidence of cancer when the pathologist did his "slice and dice" in the laboratory. After checking the blood test three more times and finding the HCG still grossly elevated, her doctors had insisted on another round of chemo. A different cocktail of medications this time, hopefully to eradicate the cancer that was slowly killing her.

The nurse adjusted the flow on the intake valve of the IV tubing. She stared down at Andrea, said a quick prayer for her, and made the sign of the cross as she crept out of the room.

Andrea opened her eyes. If only she believed in miracles. But she didn't. There was no doubt in her mind that she was dying.

She wanted to believe in God, to find the strength and solace so many people found in religion. But she'd always been a non-believer. She was too much of a realist. She saw things as black or white, right or wrong, and no in-between.

Stephanie Grimes, Andrea's roommate, arms laden with a small TV/DVD player and a Wal-Mart bag, burst into the room. "Hey, wake up! I've got goodies," she said as she set everything down on the bedside table.

Andrea smiled. "What are you doing here? You're supposed to be catching some z's. You have to work tonight."

"I slept three hours. I used to get by on a lot less in college. Anyway, I knew if I left you alone you'd be having all kinds of morbid thoughts about dying and such—which I've told you is not going to happen."

"Where did you get the little TV?"

"Borrowed it from a friend at work. She keeps it in her van so she doesn't strangle her kids when they go on trips. Thought you might like to watch a movie. I got one of your favorites, *You've Got Mail.*"

Tears crowded Andrea's eyes. She wasn't sure she would have survived all she'd been through without Stephanie. They'd been friends in college and kept in touch. After Andrea's parents died in an auto accident, since she had no siblings, it had been Stephanie's idea for her to move to Hilton Head to start a new life.

"I also brought popcorn and ginger ale. I know you'll probably puke it up later, but what's a movie without popcorn?"

Andrea chuckled. "That's easy enough for you to say. You're not the one doing the hurling."

"That's true. At least I didn't bring chocolate this time."

Andrea groaned. "Did you have to mention that?"

Stephanie busied herself with plugging in the TV and getting the DVD package open.

"Steph, thanks for doing this. You're right. It's hard to be alone during these blasted treatments."

"I knew if I left you on your own you'd be thinking about Michael. Like I told you before, it's better to find out what kind of a man he is now before you invest any more time in that relationship. He just doesn't cut it. You deserve much better."

"But he was so damned good looking."

"I'll give you that, but that's all he was, a pretty face. Now if we could just find you a standup guy like Tom Hanks."

Tears threatened to spill onto Andrea's cheeks. She knew, if not for Steph, she probably would have already swallowed a handful of pills or driven her car into a tree.

Chapter Three

Marissa Langford stood back from the canvas and surveyed the oil painting she'd been working on for the past six weeks. She'd been taking art classes for almost a year, and, although Marissa was no Van Gogh, her instructor said she had natural talent.

Raindrops pinged on the skylight as she daubed a little more white onto the tops of the waves. In the painting, the boat rocked precariously as a man, whose fishing pole was bent at a ninety-degree angle, concentrated on bringing in a large fish, its dorsal fin barely visible above the water. The white jagged scar on the man's right cheek contrasted sharply against his tan face.

Detective "Shark" Morgan, the fisherman in the painting, had shown her multiple acts of kindness after her husband, Marcus DeSilva, was murdered on their wedding day. In fact, Shark was the only man who'd ever been there for her when she needed someone and who hadn't expected anything in return. Even though she'd been a suspect in her husband's death, he'd treated her with respect, something she wasn't accustomed to.

Marissa decided she would only destroy the raw emotion the painting exhibited if she tampered with it further, so she signed her first initial and last name in the right hand corner and dropped her brush into the jar of turpentine. She crossed to the sink and washed her hands.

As she picked up the towel, she studied the canvas from across the room. She decided it was her best work yet, and felt certain Shark would be pleased if he ever had the opportunity to see it.

As she ground beans for the espresso maker, she wondered if he still worked for the Beaufort County Sheriff's Office. She knew he'd been attracted to her during the investigation, but their lives were too different for anything more than friendship to develop between them. Besides, back then she'd been counting the days until she could escape from Hilton Head Island.

Marissa picked up the mail lying on the table and began flipping through it as she waited for her coffee. She paused at an envelope addressed to Marissa DeSilva, surprised, since she'd resumed her maiden name as soon as she'd left the States. The return address on the envelope indicated it was from the lawyer handling Marcus's estate.

Marissa ripped it open, hoping to find that the probate was finally settled. She'd placed Marcus's oceanfront home, his real estate development business, his yacht, and all his other assets in the hands of James Kellum before she'd fled Hilton Head Island. She smiled at the thought of the substantial wealth that was about to become hers.

But as she skimmed the letter, her forehead wrinkled. Diane DeSilva, Marcus's first wife and mother of his son, BJ, was contesting the will. BJ had died in an auto accident a few weeks after his father's murder, and his mother felt that she was entitled to his share of the estate. There was a hearing scheduled in ten days at the courthouse in Beaufort, South Carolina, where Marissa would have to appear.

Marissa balled up the letter and threw it across the room. *What a bunch of bull! Marcus's will specifically stated that if something happened to BJ, I was to inherit his entire estate. Who does that woman think she is? They'd been divorced for years. And what makes her think she can contest the will after this period of time?*

Marissa glanced at the clock, calculating the time difference, then went in search of her address book. She didn't care what time it was in South Carolina, she had to talk to James Kellum. There was no way she was going to return to the Lowcountry if there was a way she could get out of it. Even though she'd been cleared of her husband's murder, she knew there were some people, including Shark's partner, who still felt she was somehow involved.

Dell Hassler yawned as she dunked the Constant Comment teabag into the steaming mug of water on her desk. She'd felt nauseated when she got up this morning and hadn't been able to stomach the thought of coffee, so she'd missed her usual pick-me-up to get Monday morning at the office off the ground. Even though she'd gotten a solid seven hours of sleep, she still felt tired, and the lack of caffeine was giving her a headache. Glad that she and her partner had driven separate cars this morning, she wondered how Shark's dentist appointment was going. She knew he caved in only if he was having a major problem.

An hour later, Detective William "Shark" Morgan strode in carrying a cup of coffee, and the smell of it almost made Dell gag.

Shark spotted the Ziploc baggie filled with tea bags lying on her desk. "You're not drinking coffee? What gives?"

"My stomach just feels a little queasy. I thought maybe the tea would help settle it."

"You do look a little green around the gills. Big weekend?"

"No, I think I might be getting a flu bug or something, so you might want to keep your distance. How did you get along at the dentist?"

Shark set his coffee on the desk and pulled off his sport coat. "With all the technology we have today you'd think they could come up with a painless way to numb a tooth. At least the Novocaine is starting to wear off."

"So are you a state record-holder?" Dell asked. She knew Shark and her sister-in-law, Jazz, had planned to fish in a tournament over the weekend.

"Hardly. I didn't even get to see Jazz. She called Friday evening just as I was getting ready to head to Charleston and said she was covered up with paperwork for an important trial next week."

"So what'd you do all weekend?"

"Messed around in the yard, worked on my Mustang. My neighbor, Gary, and I went fishing yesterday. But you'll never guess who called me last night."

"I haven't a clue."

Shark leaned back in his chair and propped his feet on the desk. "I'll give you a hint. The call was from Paris."

Dell scrunched up her forehead. "Who do you know in Paris?"

"We both know this person."

Dell rolled her eyes. "Enough all ready, just tell me."

"Okay, okay. Marissa DeSilva."

"For heaven's sake. Why did she call you? Tell me you haven't been communicating with her!" Dell had no use for the woman who'd almost destroyed her partner's career.

Shark raised his hands. "No, I swear. I think she called because she was pissed and couldn't get hold of her lawyer. It seems Diane DeSilva is contesting Marcus's will, and Marissa has to appear at the hearing in Beaufort in a few days. She was asking me all kinds of legal questions I couldn't answer. Anyway, she said she's been living in Paris and taking art classes and flying lessons."

Dell wrapped both hands around her mug of tea. "Well just don't go getting involved with her again."

Shark lowered his feet and picked up a report off his desk. He glanced back over at Dell, studying her. He couldn't believe she hadn't reacted more to his call from Marissa. Usually the mention of Marissa's name sent Dell off on a rampage. And she looked tired and pale. He suddenly blurted out, "Hey, are you pregnant?"

Dell's head snapped up. "No, of course not. I'm on the pill, and I haven't missed a single one."

"Are you sure? I've heard of people getting pregnant on the pill."

"That only happens if you don't take them right, or take antibiotics or something." The words were hardly out of her mouth before she realized she'd been on penicillin for an impacted wisdom tooth a couple of weeks ago. But she'd started her period yesterday, so surely she didn't have anything to worry about.

"Yeah, but weren't you . . ."

"Just shut up, okay? I'm not pregnant. Let's get to work."

Shark decided to drop the subject. The phone shrilled on his desk interrupting their conversation.

"Morgan here."

He listened for a moment and made a note. "We're on our way."

He turned to Dell. "We've got a body in Bluffton."

As they exited the Beaufort County Sheriff's satellite office on Lagoon Road on the south end of Hilton Head Island, the August heat and humidity enveloped them.

Dell buckled her seat belt. "I heard on the news this morning that it's supposed to get to a hundred and two today."

"Great. I don't think the temperature in my house got below eighty last night. The AC never shut off."

"I know what you mean. Can you imagine living down here in the days before air conditioning?"

"I think I would have headed north for Yankee country," Shark said as he entered the traffic on Pope Avenue.

Twenty minutes later, they pulled into the driveway of a small brick house on Burnt Church Road in Bluffton. Deputy Sayles greeted them as they exited their vehicle. A short distance away, a female officer from the Bluffton Police Department was interviewing an elderly woman.

The body of a middle-aged man was slumped over the steering wheel of a black Honda Accord. Deputy Sayles flipped open his notebook. "Art Grimes. Neighbor lady over there saw him early this morning when she went to the mailbox for her newspaper. Said she thought he was sleeping it off. Seems he's a heavy drinker. But when she went to let the dog out a couple of hours later, she noticed he hadn't moved. So she walked over to see if he was okay. That's when she saw all the blood and called it in."

"Did she touch anything?" Shark asked as he glanced over at the car.

"She said she didn't."

"I bet you a buck she touched either the car door or the body."

Sayles shook his head. "I'll pass on that bet."

Shark was pulling on a pair of latex gloves when he saw the coroner's car grind to a halt a short distance away. Grabbing her bag, Anna Connors strode briskly toward the crime scene.

"I was hoping we wouldn't get any calls today," she said as she wiped the sweat off her brow with the back of her hand. "Have you swept the scene?"

"Not yet. We just got here. Give me a minute," Shark said as he pulled a magnifying glass out of his pocket.

Shark and Dell got down on all fours and slowly worked their way toward the vehicle. They bagged four cigarette butts, three hairs, and a crushed beer can before they cleared a large enough area for the coroner to approach. Shark lifted the door handle with a pen, careful not to smudge any prints that might remain.

After a cursory exam, Anna said, "Looks like one gunshot wound to the head, probably a thirty-eight. He appears to have been in a fight just prior to his death. He has a broken nose and cut lip. Won't know about internal injuries until we open him up."

"TOD?" Shark asked.

"I'd estimate somewhere between one and four A.M. They can probably pin it down closer on autopsy."

An ambulance pulled in behind the coroner's car, and two men jumped out and began to unload the gurney.

Anxious to get out of the heat, Shark snapped pictures of the crime scene while Dell completed the sweep.

"Looks like the shooter crept up behind the driver's door and shot from about a foot away," Anna said. "From the angle of the entry wound, I'd say our guy was draped over the steering wheel, much as you see him now, either drunk or asleep. Since the car window was down, someone just reached in and wham! Shot him right over the brain stem area."

"Are you saying the shooter may know something about anatomy?" Shark asked.

"Not necessarily. It could have just been the way the victim's head was turned."

Dell groaned and grabbed her back as she stood up. "I'm finished here. Didn't get much. Want to hand me his keys so I can start inside?"

"You just want to get out of the heat," Shark said as he opened the passenger door, leaned in, and removed the ring of keys.

"My mama didn't raise no fool," Dell said as she snatched them out of his hand and headed for the house.

When Shark entered the residence thirty minutes later, the body was on its way to Charleston. At first, he just walked through the three-bedroom house to get a feel for their victim. Mr. Grimes appeared to live alone. The kitchen sink was full of dirty dishes, hardly any food in the refrigerator, and no signs of any female touches.

Shark stuck his head in the master bedroom where Dell was working and noted the piles of dirty clothes strewn about the room. The next room he entered contained cardboard packing boxes but not much else. It made Shark wonder how long Grimes had lived there. From the inch-thick dust on the top of the boxes, it appeared he'd been there for a while.

In the next bedroom, Shark was surprised to find a relatively clean room. The bed was made, and a few casual shirts hung in the closet along with two pairs of khakis. They appeared to be a size larger and of a much better quality than the jeans and T-shirts he'd seen in the master bedroom. Shark walked through the door that connected to the bathroom shared by both of the smaller bedrooms. Clean towels were folded neatly, and the sink was clean. He finished his sweep of the rooms and returned to the master bedroom. Dell was going through the nightstand. "I found a pay stub in a kitchen drawer. Looks like he worked for Tri County Builders. But I haven't located an address book yet. Can you believe this filth? How do people live like this?"

"Beats me. I think he has a roommate. The third bedroom

was pretty clean, and the clothes in the closet look too big for our vic."

"I haven't made it that far yet. Did you notice there are no photos or personal items sitting around?"

"Maybe they're still in the boxes in the second bedroom."

"You want to start looking in there while I finish here?"

"I can do that."

As Shark turned to leave, Deputy Sayles stuck his head in the door.

"I interviewed the neighbors. Seems like Grimes has lived here about six months, worked for a construction company, and pretty much kept to himself. A couple of nights a week another car appears with an older man who stays all night. There's been some talk in the neighborhood they might be lovers. The woman in the second house down said she thought the car had Florida tags and was a dark green Buick, but she wasn't real sure. The lady who found him, Mrs. Greenfield, said Grimes was a heavy drinker. She would observe him staggering to his front door late at night on weekends and sometimes see him drinking beer on the back patio when she'd walk her dog. That's about it."

"Thanks, Sayles. Dell and I'll take it from here."

"Is the officer from the city police department still interviewing people?" Dell asked.

"No, she got another call so she left about fifteen minutes ago. Catch you later," Sayles said as he turned and headed down the hallway.

The detectives spent an additional two hours before they felt they had gleaned all they were going to from the scene. They locked the doors securely and strung crime scene tape across them before heading out.

Shark cranked the AC up to max and pulled onto Burnt Church Road.

"We didn't get much from the scene," Dell said as she fanned herself with her notebook.

"Yeah, and you look about as bad as the vic. Are you sure you're okay?"

Dell turned her head and looked out the window. "I think it's just the heat."

Chapter Four

"Ears" McCannum slipped his headphones around his neck and turned off the tape recorder. He rolled his wheelchair over to the telephone and dialed a number in California. He wasn't looking forward to the conversation he was about to have.

Devon Phillips recognized the international number on his cell phone display. He smiled in anticipation of the news he was about to hear.

"Is it done?" Devon asked.

Ears picked up his glass of wine and took a sip. "A little complication."

"What kind of complication?" Devon demanded.

"The package is still walking around and headed back to the States. She has to appear in court in a few days. Something to do with her husband's will. Plus she had a conversation with a cop in South Carolina."

Devon let loose a string of obscenities.

Ears filled him in on the debacle with the shooting, glad he hadn't been the one responsible for the screwup.

"I don't like her talking to that cop. Put a tail on her while she's in South Carolina. As for the other matter, I'll take care of that myself—what I should have done in the first place."

"You want me to keep monitoring her phone calls?" Ears asked.

17

"Absolutely. I want to know if she has any more little chats with the cop."

Ears grabbed his Rolodex. "I'll take care of the tail."

As soon as they returned to the office, Dell immediately sat down at her computer and typed in their victim's name. Shark picked up the telephone to call Tri County Builders.

After a brief conversation with a sexy-voiced receptionist, he located where the crew was working and headed out to talk to the foreman.

When Shark returned two hours later, Dell had computer printouts covering her desk.

"I didn't learn much. How about you?" he asked as he plopped down in his chair.

"Well, Grimes has an interesting history."

"Really?"

"Yes. About fifteen years ago, he was arrested and charged with manslaughter in the death of his wife. But when it went to trial, he was found not guilty. Seems the jury felt it was an accident."

"What happened?" Shark asked as he leaned over to tie his shoelace.

"He and his wife were having an argument. He said she lunged at him with a steak knife, and when he moved to get out of the way, she tripped and fell and hit her head on the fireplace hearth and died. The police had been called twice previously to the residence to break up fights between the two, but she didn't have any fresh bruises or anything on autopsy to indicate that he'd hit her that night. His twelve-year-old daughter testified at the hearing that he frequently beat her mother, but the night of the accident, she was staying at a friend's house. There was a younger brother who was home, but they didn't put him on the stand. Must have thought he didn't see anything or was too young to testify. A couple of years later, old Art was arrested for fondling a ten-year-old neighbor boy, but the charges were dropped, and he never went to trial."

"The parents probably didn't want to put their child through the nasty ordeal of describing everything in open court."

"He'd also been arrested for two DUIs and assault and battery for a bar fight."

"Sounds like he didn't have a whole lot of redeeming qualities. So did you learn where the son and daughter live so we can notify them of their father's death and find out where they were last night? Maybe they harbored a grudge all these years and decided to take justice into their own hands."

"I just located the daughter about five minutes before you walked in. Seems she lives on the island here, at Marshside Villas. Haven't tracked down the son yet."

"Think that's why Grimes moved to Bluffton, to be near his daughter?"

Dell grabbed her purse out of the bottom desk drawer. "Let's go find out."

Once they were in the car, Dell asked, "So what did you learn from his boss?"

"Not much. He was a trim man, did all the crown moldings and such. Kept to himself most of the time. He'd been warned about showing up late and missing a day occasionally. Nobody on the crew seemed to know much about him. Most of the employees were Hispanic, so I didn't get very far with them."

"Since the neighbors thought he may be gay, do you think it could be a hate crime?" Dell asked.

"That's always a possibility. Maybe we can learn more when the roommate shows up. At least he can tell us if there'd been any threats."

A few minutes later, they pulled into the parking lot of Marshside, a condominium complex on the north end of the island, and drove around until they located the correct address.

Andrea sat on the cold tile floor of the bathroom hugging the toilet bowl. She'd been throwing up every few minutes since she'd returned home after completing her treatment. She laid her head down on the pillow on the floor to rest until the next wave of nausea hit. She tried to be as quiet as possible, since her roommate was getting a little rest before she had to go to work. Finally, she couldn't stand the foul taste in her mouth any longer, so she stood up and leaned against the sink for support as she tried to brush her teeth, but she kept gagging. She stared at the face in the mirror. Her eyebrows were gone, and she'd already started losing patches of hair, so she knew it wouldn't be long before the remainder fell out. She was tired of this, the constant weakness, feelings of nausea, losing her hair. And for what purpose? A few more weeks to grace the earth?

Her thoughts were interrupted by the insistent ringing of the doorbell. She quickly rinsed her mouth and placed her toothbrush back in the holder. She hoped to get to the door before the noise woke Stephanie.

Shark and Dell were not prepared for the tall, ill-looking woman who answered the door. She was dressed in a pair of mint-green sweats, a washcloth pressed to her forehead, bald spots the size of half dollars all over her scalp. The detectives tried not to stare.

Shark was the first to recover. He pulled out his badge and introduced himself. "Are you Stephanie Grimes?" he asked.

"No, Stephanie's my roommate. She's asleep. What's this all about?" Andrea asked as she leaned on the doorframe for support.

"We need to speak to Miss Grimes. Would you wake her up please?" Shark asked.

Andrea motioned for them to enter and have a seat in the living room. She staggered down the hall and knocked on Stephanie's bedroom door, then slipped quietly into the room.

She leaned over the bed and nudged Stephanie on the shoulder. "Hey, wake up."

Stephanie groaned, then turned over and stretched her arms over her head. "I'm awake. What do you need? Are you sick again?"

"There are some cops here who want to talk to you."

"Cops?" Stephanie said, sitting up in bed. "Why do they want to talk to me?"

"I don't know. They just asked me to wake you up."

"It must have something to do with the office. Maybe somebody's been stealing or something." She quickly pulled up the long white T-shirt she'd been sleeping in, picked up a pair of khaki shorts off the floor, and slipped into them.

She ran her hands through her shoulder-length red hair as she walked down the hall. Andrea followed silently, still clutching the washcloth to her forehead.

As Stephanie entered the room, Shark and Dell stood up. "Are you Stephanie Grimes?" Shark asked.

"Yes. What's this all about?" Stephanie glanced at the badge Shark flashed in her direction.

"I'm Detective William Morgan, and this is my partner, Dell Hassler. I think you should have a seat, Miss Grimes."

Stephanie lowered herself into the rocking chair, and Andrea sat down on the footstool, as the detectives resumed their positions on the couch.

"I'm sorry, but I'm afraid we have some bad news. Your father, Art Grimes, is dead," Shark said softly.

"Bad news?" Stephanie blurted out as she jumped up from her chair. "It's the best news I've heard in a long time!"

In view of what she'd learned about Stephanie's father, Dell wasn't surprised by Stephanie's reaction. "So I take it you two didn't have a good relationship?"

"We've had no relationship since he murdered my mother."

"But the jury found him not guilty, that her death was an accident," Shark said as he watched her begin to pace in the tiny room.

"I don't care what they said. He killed her as sure as I'm standing here."

"And what do you base that on?" Dell asked.

"History. He used to beat her all the time. He had an explosive temper, especially when he was drunk. And my brother, Brent, was home that night. He heard Dad threaten her."

"Did he ever hit you or your brother?" Shark asked.

"Occasionally, but most of the time he'd lock us in the closet for hours while he beat on Mom. There was a lot of psychological abuse. He'd make us remain silent during meals, take our plates away if we uttered a sound. If he was sober, which was rare, things would be pretty normal for an evening. But if he'd been drinking, we never knew what to expect. It was maddening to wait each day for him to get home from work, not sure which it would be. When I got a little older and my body began to change, he started leering at me and making crude comments. Then, just a couple of days before Mom died, he barged into my bedroom and said he wanted to tuck me in. He kissed me on the mouth."

"Did you tell your mother?" Dell asked.

"No. He said if I did, he'd kill her and Brent, but I think she knew. It's all my fault she died. I should have been there that night."

"It's not your fault. You were only twelve years old," Shark said. "What kind of relationship did you and he have after the trial?" Shark asked.

"None. Social Services placed me and my brother with my maternal grandparents, and we refused to even talk to him."

"Did you have any contact with him after he moved to Bluffton?" Dell asked.

Stephanie shook her head. "No, he called here several times and left messages on the answering machine, but I never returned them. One morning he tried to approach me in the parking lot at the Westin Hotel where I work, but I just got in the car and drove off. Another time he showed up here, but I wasn't home. I didn't even know he lived in Bluffton."

Andrea's stomach began to churn, and she knew she was going to be sick again. She stood up and practically ran down the hallway.

"Is your roommate all right?" Dell asked.

"That depends on how you define it. No, she's not all right. She's undergoing her second round of chemotherapy for cancer. She just had a treatment today, and she usually pukes for the next twenty-four to thirty-six hours."

"I'm sorry," Dell said. "She's looks so young."

"She's only twenty-seven."

"Back to your father," Shark gently interrupted. "You said you didn't even know he lived in Bluffton?"

"That's correct."

"And you never called him on the telephone or anything?"

"Absolutely not."

"Not even to tell him to quit bothering you?"

Stephanie turned to Shark. "No. Like I told you, I haven't talked to him since I was twelve."

Dell pulled a notepad out of her purse. "So where were you last night?"

"At work from eleven to seven." With a look of surprise, Stephanie asked, "You mean you think it wasn't natural causes?"

"No, he was shot," Shark said as he watched her expression.

Stephanie stopped pacing, returned to her chair, and collapsed into it. "Serves him right! When did it happen?"

"Early this morning. You didn't leave work at all last night?" Shark asked.

"No, and like I said before, I didn't even know where he lived."

"Do you own a gun?" Dell asked.

"No."

"Where does your brother live?" Shark asked.

"In Savannah. But I'm sure he had nothing to do with it. He hasn't seen Dad either."

"We need his address and phone number," Shark said.

"All I have for him is a cell phone number. He's a student at Armstrong University and is just staying with various friends and doing some housesitting this summer," Stephanie said as she moved to the desk and pulled out her address book.

As Shark was writing the phone number down, they could hear Andrea vomiting in the bathroom. "Andrea needs me. Is that all?"

"For now," Shark said as he and Dell stood up.

Stephanie hurried to the refrigerator and pulled out a box with a pharmacy label on it. She removed a foil-covered suppository. She glanced over at the detectives. "Phenergan. It helps with the nausea."

Chapter Five

"Geez, can you imagine being twenty-seven years old and having cancer?" Dell asked when they were back in the car.

"Fortunately, no."

"So what did you think about Stephanie Grimes?" she asked as she leaned over and repositioned the air conditioning vent.

"I don't think she's going to lose any sleep over her father getting shot."

"Do you really think she hasn't talked to him in all that time?"

Shark pulled out onto Gum Tree Road and drove the short distance to the red light. "I don't know. I got a feeling she wasn't being totally honest with us. Check her phone records to be sure."

"Think her mom found out about daddy tucking her in at night?"

"That would explain why she might have attacked him with a knife."

"I'll see what additional information I can come up with on our victim when we get back to the office," Dell said.

"Where did he move here from?" Shark asked as he fought the slow moving traffic on William Hilton Parkway.

"Spartanburg."

"Let's dig into his life there and see if there's anyone with a motive to kill him. Also, let's call Stephanie's brother and see when we can meet with him."

Dell took a sip from her bottle of water. "Will do."

Shark swerved into the left lane as a gray Saturn with Georgia plates made an abrupt turn into Port Royal Plaza. "Tourists," he muttered.

"I wonder how long it'll take for Grimes's roommate to show up."

"I hope it's soon. I imagine once he sees the crime scene tape across the front door, we'll get a call from him. If for no other reason than he'll want to get his things out of the house."

Dell reached for her sunglasses. "I think we need to have the locks changed since he has a key, so he doesn't remove his things before we get a chance to talk to him."

"Good idea. Can you handle that once we get back?"

"I'll do that first thing."

Shark stopped at the light in front of Shipyard Plantation. "Is Wendy's drive-thru okay with you for dinner? I think we're going to be here for awhile."

"That's fine, but I just want a baked potato."

Shark glanced over at her. "Stomach still not feeling good?"

"No, but I feel hungry."

Shark just grinned.

Andrea lay in bed, a cold washcloth on her forehead. The Phenergan suppository was making her drowsy. Stephanie walked in with a glass of ice chips and sat down on the side of the bed.

"Want some of these?"

"Just a few. I'm afraid I'll start vomiting again, but the medicine is making my mouth feel like a desert. So are you okay?"

"I'm fine. It's not like I had a relationship with the man anymore. In my eyes, he died when he killed my mother. I only wish I'd had the courage to send him on his way years ago."

Andrea placed a few ice chips in the washcloth and readjusted it on her forehead. "So you have no regrets about not meeting with him or returning his calls?"

Stephanie grabbed the worn brown teddy bear off the bed and hugged it to her chest. "What was there to say? Even if he'd apologized for how he treated us and admitted that he'd killed her and was sorry, it would have been too late. I still wouldn't have wanted anything to do with him."

"Why did you tell the police you hadn't seen him?"

"I don't know. It was out of my mouth before I realized it—and then it was too late to change my story. It would have seemed suspicious."

"Who do you think shot him?"

Stephanie shook her head. "I have no idea, but whoever did, God bless them. I just pray it wasn't Brent. I only hope I can get in touch with him before the cops do. I tried his phone but didn't get an answer."

Andrea yawned.

"Let's both of us try to get some sleep. I don't think my boss will understand if he finds me nodding off at my computer tonight," Stephanie said as she stood up and made sure the plastic lined wastebasket was within Andrea's reach. "I'll check on you in a couple of hours. If you need something before then just give me a holler."

Stephanie left her bedroom door open so she would be able to hear Andrea if she called out. She slipped her shorts off, pulled back the sheet, and lay on her back with her hands behind her head.

So he was dead. It was about time. He had all those extra years that her mother never had the opportunity to enjoy. She hadn't been perfectly honest with the police. She *had* talked to him, even threatened to kill him.

He'd started calling three months ago. At first, just a couple of messages on their answering machine. Then somehow, he'd gotten her cell phone number. The first time she answered and heard his voice, she'd been stunned. She hung up without saying anything. After that, she began to screen her calls. He filled her voice mail with multiple messages about how he needed to talk to her and see her. At first, she just ignored them. Then he'd begun to follow her. The first time she'd become aware of it was when she walked out of the beauty shop and saw him leaning against his car. She'd raced to her vehicle and locked the door. By the time she was backing out of her parking spot, he was pounding on her trunk.

She'd been petrified. Why had he come back? To kill her too? She'd driven around the island until she was sure she'd lost him before she returned home. She'd run in the door and collapsed into tears as she recounted what had happened to Andrea.

Since then she'd been looking over her shoulder wherever she went. And it had begun to wear on her. Then it finally happened. On a recent morning when she got off work, he'd accosted her in the parking lot. He'd grabbed her by the arm and tried to drag her to his car. He kept insisting all he wanted to do was talk to her.

She'd fought like a wild woman, kicking and biting until she freed herself, then darted into the underground parking garage where she hid until he left.

By the time she got home, she was hysterical. After she calmed down enough to explain to Andrea what had happened, Andrea was concerned he was going to kidnap her or hurt her and had insisted she contact the police and file a restraining order against him. But since he hadn't really threatened her, she wasn't sure the cops would take any action.

A few days later, when she exited the dry cleaners, his car was parked next to hers. She'd had enough. She leaned through his window and told him that if he didn't quit following her, she would kill him. Just like he'd killed her mother. That she carried a pistol and knew how to use it.

He hadn't said a word, just stared at her. However, he promptly started the car and made a quick retreat. That was the last time she'd seen him.

When she got home and shared the story with Andrea, they'd both laughed. She didn't even own a gun.

Now it was over. She could sleep in peace. But as she drifted off she wondered if her father had attempted to contact Brent like he had her. She hadn't talked to Brent since she'd told him about their father following her. She'd try to call him again when she got up.

Chapter Six

Shark lay in bed naked. Even though the ceiling fan was on high, it simply moved the warm air around the room. When he'd checked the thermostat an hour before, it still read close to eighty. Either he needed to invest in additional insulation for the attic or a more powerful air conditioner.

Something was going on with Jazz. He'd sensed it the past few weeks but couldn't put his finger on what had changed in their relationship. He wanted to ask her about it but was afraid he might not like what she had to say. They'd been dating for a year and a half, and he'd asked Jazz to marry him several times, but she always said she wasn't ready yet. She'd been divorced only a couple of years, but he was ready to make a commitment and start a family.

He wondered if a man was allowed only one true love, and if so, his beloved Laura had been it. He hadn't counted on melanoma stealing her away from him so quickly. He'd been so sure he and Jazz had a future together. But he'd noticed that recently it would take her a couple of days to return his phone calls, and he didn't buy the excuse that she had to work all last weekend. Maybe he was destined to spend the rest of his life alone. If so, did he want to waste those years in this house in Beaufort, South Carolina?

For the past few years, he'd fantasized about moving to Key West after he retired and starting a fishing charter business. Unfortunately, that was years away.

Shark picked up his cigarettes and lighter off the night-stand and felt his way through the dark house to the sliding glass door in the living room. He stepped out onto the patio. The concrete was still warm on his bare feet, and the heat and humidity still hung heavy in the air. He wasn't prepared for the dew as his naked backside sank onto the metal chair.

He clicked his lighter and took a long drag on his ciga-rette. The moon was full, and he could hear cicadas singing close by. At least if he was out on his boat, he might be able to catch some ocean breeze. Maybe that's what he should do, sell his house and buy a boat big enough to live on. He'd talked about it for years but felt that if he and Jazz did get married, she probably wouldn't like the idea of a floating home. But that might never happen. Maybe he should seri-ously think about the boat idea. He could avoid that killer drive every day to the island. Palmetto Bay Marina and Outdoor Resorts both allowed live-aboards.

He cleared his throat as he threw his cigarette butt into the grass.

"That you, Shark?"

"Yeah, Gary, it's me." Shark couldn't see his neighbor over the high wooden fence.

"Got a cool one over here if you want to walk over."

"Can't, I'm naked."

"Won't bother me, but Sheila might be a little embar-rassed."

Sheila started giggling. "Hell, I'm sitting here in my skimpy gown, won't bother me."

"On second thought, why don't I just pass you one over the fence," Gary said.

"Won't argue with that," Shark said as he stood up.

As he grabbed the cold can he said, "What would you say if I told you I was thinking about putting the old place up for sale and buying a big-assed boat to live on?"

"I'd wonder what took you so long. If I was single, I sure as hell would consider it."

"Watch out there, cowboy," Sheila said.

"Just make sure it's got an extra bunk for me," Gary said as he walked back over and sat down.

Shark popped the tab and drank thirstily, then lit another cigarette. He had stopped smoking off and on the last couple of years, mostly at Jazz's insistence. After she canceled their plans for the weekend, he'd stopped and bought a pack.

He thought more about living on a boat and could see several advantages. Besides avoiding the heavy traffic on the drive each morning, he could throw a fishing line over the side whenever he wanted. Or move out into Port Royal Sound in the evenings if he wanted to do some serious fishing. A boat big enough to live on would have air conditioning and all the amenities. But if he sold his house, could he afford it? He wondered how much the dock fee would be each month. He had about $50,000 equity in his house, which would give him a down payment. He could sell his other boat and the old pickup truck he hauled it around with and just keep his Mustang. But there was always maintenance with a boat, especially one left in the water all the time. The salt water was hard on them. Well . . . he didn't have to make a decision tonight.

Shark drained the last drop from the beer can. "Thanks for the brew," he yelled over to Gary. "Think I'll head to bed."

"Don't let the bed bugs bite," Sheila said.

Rebecca Sands pulled into the crowded parking lot of the Beaufort County Sheriff's office. She shut off the engine and adjusted the rearview mirror so she could touch up her lipstick. Then she grabbed her notepad and pen and headed into the office.

The man seated behind the check-in area, dressed in civilian clothes, asked, "Can I help you?"

Putting on her best smile and flashing the teeth that had cost her father a fortune, Rebecca said, "I need to speak to Detective William Morgan."

"Can I tell him what it's about?"

"The Art Grimes investigation."

"Have a seat in the waiting area, and I'll see if he's in. Your name?"

"Rebecca Sands."

Rebecca was too nervous to have a seat, so she paced instead.

Shark and Dell were reviewing the autopsy report on Art Grimes when the phone on his desk rang. He listened for a moment, then said, "I'll be right out." He turned to Dell. "Some lady's here who wants to talk about Art Grimes."

"Great. We need all the help we can get."

Shark walked down the hall and opened the door to the lobby. He saw a woman in her early thirties with short blond hair. She was dressed in a coral-colored silk blouse and a white skirt that struck her just above the knees. A pair of white two-inch heels drew attention to her long suntanned legs. "Ms. Sands?"

"Yes," she said, offering her hand.

Shark was surprised by the firmness of her handshake. "Right this way."

Neither said anything as he led her to his office. "This is my partner, Dell Hassler. Have a seat."

Rebecca sat down in the proffered chair. Once Shark had resumed his place at his desk, he turned to her and said, "I understand you have some information about Art Grimes."

Rebecca put her best smile in place again. "Actually, I'm a new reporter for *The Island Packet*. I just moved here from Atlanta where I did some investigative reporting for *The Atlanta Journal*. I worked their crime beat and had a good relationship with the police department there."

Shark looked down at the floor and tried to keep the irritation out of his voice. "So what do you know about Art Grimes?"

"No more than what I read in the newspaper this morning. That's why I'm here. I'm hopeful we can work together. I thought perhaps if we shared our resources it might bring a quicker resolution to the case."

Shark jumped up from his chair. "I don't know how things worked in Atlanta, but we don't 'share resources' down here. And for future reference, I have no use for the press, so don't think you can be mucking around with our investigation."

"Shark, cool it," Dell said as she stood up. "Unless you have some valuable information for us, I'll show you out."

Rebecca rose. "Not yet, but I intend to find out everything there is to know about Art Grimes, so don't say I didn't offer to work with you. They must call you Shark because you have about as much personality as one."

Dell hurried the reporter through the door before Shark could attack her.

He was cussing and dumping two Tums into his hand from the giant bottle he kept in his desk drawer when Dell returned.

"Calm down. She's new. You've got to give her credit for trying. But the woman must have no sweat glands. She looked like she'd just stepped out of a Cosmo ad. And I know for a fact that's a Liz Claiborne blouse, probably the skirt too. Did you see that big rock on her ring finger? I practically needed my sunglasses. I bet the only reason she moved down here is because her fiancé lives here. Why else would you go from working for *The Atlanta Journal* to *The Island Packet*?"

Shark shook his head. "I can't believe you noticed all that in the short time she was in here. That's why women give better descriptions than men."

"You didn't see or hear anything once you found out she was from the press."

"No need to."

"I'm not sure I agree with you. If she's been an investigative reporter and worked the crime beat, it might not hurt to at least treat her civilly."

"You treat her any way you want, but just keep her out of my way."

Dell sat back down at her desk and picked up the autopsy report. "This says the murder weapon was a .38 Smith & Wesson. I've done a search, and Stephanie Grimes doesn't have a gun permit, and there's no evidence that she ever purchased a gun."

"Doesn't mean she couldn't buy one on the street or get one from a friend."

"It's kinda ironic that the guy had pancreatic cancer and only a few months to live."

Shark scratched his chin. "Maybe that's why he wanted to talk to his daughter. Make things right before he met The Maker. You still haven't gotten hold of Brent Grimes?"

"I've tried several times, but there's been no answer."

"Think he's not answering his phone because he's afraid we'll call?" Shark asked.

"I spoke with Stephanie, and she said she hasn't been able to get in touch with him either. Maybe he's out of town."

"Kind of suspicious, don't you think? He disappears right after his father is shot. Let's get a class schedule from the college and try to intercept him there."

"According to Stephanie, he's not taking any classes this summer. That's why he's not living in the dorm like normal. Just bunking with friends and housesitting."

"Well, keep trying his cell phone."

Dell flipped through the papers on her desk. "I don't see a report on the trace evidence. You got it over there?"

"No, it's not back yet, but I'll be surprised if it tells us anything. Those cigarette butts were probably his, and the hairs could have been from anyone. I'm gonna get some coffee. Want some?"

"It's too hot for coffee. Grab me a diet soda."

Shark had just left the room when his phone rang. Dell hurried over, picked it up, and immediately began making notes on a pad. A couple of minutes later she disconnected then punched in another number.

When Shark returned, he heard Dell say, "Have him pick us up at Palmetto Bay Marina ASAP."

"What's up?" he asked as he handed her the cold can of soda.

"Some fishermen came across a deserted boat a few miles off South Beach, close to the Savannah ship channel. They noticed some stains on the deck that appear to be blood. I called Marine Patrol and told them to pick us up, so let's go."

"Got any sunscreen? We're gonna need it."

Chapter Seven

Andrea sat at the kitchen table transcribing a tape from Dr. Harrison's office. She felt a little better. Before she'd started doing medical transcription, she'd never thought about all the intimate details the person transcribing the tapes learned about the patient. Most of the time it was boring, routine visits, but occasionally she would learn who was suffering from sexual dysfunction due to his blood pressure medicine, who had cheated on his wife and contracted a sexually transmitted disease, and who was a closet homosexual and requested medication to treat the depression associated with it. Then there were the women physically abused by their spouses, or ones who had an alcohol or depression problem. She and Stephanie had been waiting for a table at Cracker Barrel one Sunday morning when they announced that Mr. Arsaka's table of four was ready. She recognized the unusual name immediately and could have spieled off his medical problems, but she didn't. One of the first things she'd learned when she worked in a general practitioner's office in college was confidentiality.

The phone rang, interrupting her thoughts. She lunged for it before it woke up Stephanie.

"Hello."

"Andrea, this is Jill, Dr. Bartholomeu's nurse. How you doing today?"

"Better, thanks. I've stopped vomiting."

"Good. Doc just wanted me to call and see if you were able to keep any food down yet."

"I had some chicken noodle soup for lunch, and so far so good."

"Great. Drink plenty of Gatorade to replace the electrolytes you lose when vomiting."

"Sure thing."

"You're halfway through this cycle now, only three more treatments. Doc wants you to come in next week so he can check your white blood count. And try to stay away from anyone who's sick."

"I know the drill. I'll see you then."

Andrea hung up the phone. She was tired of all the blood tests and x-rays and being mercilessly gouged when they had trouble getting an IV started. She was ready to chuck it all and make the best use of her time before the end came.

She wondered what death would be like. She didn't believe in an after-life. She figured hell was right here on earth. And when the time got close, and the pain became too much, she hoped she would have the nerve to end it on her own time schedule. With that end in mind, she'd begun to hoard a stash of pain pills.

Life didn't seem fair. Why should she get cancer at such an early age and never have an opportunity to be married and have a child? Being a mother was something she'd dreamed of since she used to play with her dolls. She'd had so many grand plans about living in a big house on the ocean, having a wonderful husband and a slew of kids. She'd never aspired to have a high profile career, just to be a good wife and mother.

But she would be denied the opportunity to experience the close bond with a man, like the one her mother had shared with her father. They'd always seemed so happy. As their only child, she'd been her mother's princess ballerina, and her father's surrogate son.

Her mother had sewn all her beautiful dancing costumes, and her father had taken her on hunting and fishing excursions. He used to tease her about being able to hit a paper target but always missing the real game. She remembered the one and only time she'd proven him wrong, the frightening morning when her father stepped into a large rut, twisting his ankle, and falling to the ground. Suddenly a wild pig came charging out of a nearby stand of trees. As she watched the animal bear down on her father, she'd fired her rifle, dropping the pig a few feet away. Oh how she missed her parents.

If only Michael hadn't left when he did, maybe she could've had the opportunity to be a wife and experience motherhood. But it was too late for that now.

Rebecca Sands was pissed. She hadn't expected the detectives to roll out the red carpet for her, but she had anticipated being treated in a more professional manner. After all, who did they think they were dealing with, some country bumpkin? She'd spent three years on the crime desk and probably knew as much, or more, than they did about investigating a murder.

She took the exit off Highway 278 onto I-95 and set the cruise control on her yellow Firebird convertible. It was a long drive to Spartanburg. She had the top up and the air conditioner on max.

Shark, what kind of name was that? A real sleazeball, she thought as she grabbed a package of cheese crackers off the passenger seat. Was he afraid a mere woman might actually contribute something to his investigation? Well, she would show him.

Rebecca was beginning to wonder if she'd made the right decision about giving up her position and moving to the island to join Hunter Cowan. Ten years her senior, he was one of the top real estate agents on the island, plus he managed a number of longterm and short-term rental properties. She'd met him at an art show in Atlanta and maintained a long distance relationship with him for the past eighteen months. Now that they were engaged, even though no date had been set, he'd begged her to move in with him. She'd declined to do so until they were married, her mama having taught her about the cow and free milk thing, but she'd agreed to move on down so they could spend more time together. She'd rented a small one-bedroom apartment at Westbury Park, just off the island.

Hunter hadn't been too happy when she'd called him after leaving the sheriff's office and canceled their date for dinner, explaining that she needed to scoot on up to Spartanburg for something she was working on. He wanted her to become a woman of leisure and spend her time volunteering in the community. He thought it would be good for his business, but she just couldn't picture herself teaching English to the Hispanic population that was coming to the island in droves, delivering meals on wheels, or answering phones at the Volunteers In Medicine clinic. She had stories to pursue and a stupid detective to best.

Deputy Russell Mitchell slid the thirty-foot Marine Patrol boat, which the department had confiscated in a drug raid, up to the dock at Palmetto Bay Marina. Shark and Dell jumped aboard, and Russ guided the boat back out into Broad Creek. The heat and humidity enveloped them. Within minutes, their clothes were as wet as if they'd stepped into a sauna.

They snaked their way through the no wake zone and cruised past million-dollar homes and private docks where an array of boats, from small skiffs to large cabin cruisers, was moored.

"How do you stand being out in this heat all day?" Dell asked as she opened the top button of her blouse and fanned herself with a map she found in one of the compartments.

"I'd rather be on the water than stuck in an office or a patrol car. Most of the time it's not too bad. But days like today are a bear."

"I'd love being out here all the time," Shark piped in.

"Yeah, but I imagine the sheriff would frown on you throwing a fishing line over the side while you were on patrol," Dell said.

"So where exactly are we headed?" Russ asked once they reached the mouth of Broad Creek.

"Savannah ship channel, near marker fifty-six. Some anglers called in an abandoned boat. Says it looks like there's some blood on the deck," Shark said.

Russ goosed the throttle up to thirty-five miles per hour, and the boat came on plane. The additional breeze, even though still warm, was welcome. They sped past more million-dollar homes in Sea Pines Plantation and the famous red and white Harbour Town lighthouse—not a real lighthouse, but one that had been built when the plantation was developed. It had rapidly become the symbol of the island since it was seen worldwide each spring when the Heritage Golf Tournament was televised. The tournament brought such a hoard of visitors that the locals tried to find somewhere to escape to for a few days. Driving the fifteen miles from one end of the island to the other during peak season could take an hour, even longer when there was a special event.

There was a mild chop on the water as they worked their way toward their destination. Conversation was difficult over the roar of the outboards. Dell was glad. She had enough trouble trying to talk the contents in her stomach into staying put.

"There's some water and sodas in the cooler," Russ yelled back to Dell. She gave him a thumbs up to let him know she'd heard him. Even though Russ had punched in the coordinates on the GPS, Shark stood next to him studying the map.

Dell watched a school of dolphins frolic off the left side of the boat until they were out of sight.

"Hey, look over there," Shark said to Russ, pointing to one of the boats off to their right. A woman had a large fish on the line, and her companion worked to get it aboard.

"Think that's a king mackerel?" Shark asked.

"Can't tell from here, but maybe. Size looks about right."

Just short of an hour from the time they'd left the dock, they reached their destination. A nineteen-foot Bayliner with two men aboard was anchored a few feet from a deserted twenty-four foot Grady White.

Shark threw out their fenders, and Russ slid up next to the Bayliner.

"Detectives Morgan and Hassler," Shark said pointing over to Dell. "Are you the one who called in the report?"

"Yes, sir," a bald-headed man said, as he removed his hat and wiped his brow with the sleeve of his shirt. "Me and my boy here came out early this morning to get in a little fishing. We noticed the boat anchored over there and figured whoever was aboard was probably sleeping down in the cabin. But as the day went along, and nobody stuck their head out, we began to get a little curious. Even if it was a couple of lovers, you'd think they would come up on deck to get some air in this heat. When we pulled our lines and decided to head in for the day, Tom thought maybe we should see if whoever was aboard was sick or something. So we headed over that way and yelled to see if anyone needed assistance, but we didn't get any answer. So we slid right up next to the boat, and that's when we saw the blood on the deck."

"Did you go aboard?" Shark asked.

"No sir. Once I saw the blood, I just got on the radio and called you guys."

"Good. That was the right thing to do. Do you recognize the boat? Ever see it out here before?"

"No. We usually fish in Port Royal Sound. Don't often venture clear out here. But we haven't been doing any good over there, so we decided to try another spot today."

"What time did you get out here this morning?" Dell asked.

"First line went in the water a little before six."

"Can you tell me your names, addresses, and phone numbers, please?" Dell said as she pulled out a notebook.

While she was recording their contact information, Shark wrote down the registration number on the side of the Grady. "I'll call that in while you and Dell are aboard," Russ said.

"Thanks."

Shark turned to the father and son. "One last question

before we let you get on your way. Did you see any other boats anchored in this vicinity today?"

"No, several came through, but nobody stopped."

"Okay. Thanks for your help. We'll call you if we have any other questions."

"Think this has got something to do with drug smuggling?" Tom asked.

"Hard to say at this point," Shark answered.

As soon as the Bayliner pulled anchor and headed for shore, Russ drove the patrol boat around the Grady White looking for any signs of damage. Nothing looked amiss. Shark took pictures from several angles.

Russ pulled up next to the Grady, and Shark tied their lines to the boat. He and Dell pulled on plastic gloves. Shark snapped pictures as best he could before they climbed aboard, careful to avoid stepping on the bloodstains on the deck. He ran through a whole roll of film before he felt he had documented the scene appropriately.

Russ was on the radio, calling in the registration number.

"I'll check the cabin," Dell said, as she opened the door and headed inside. Shark bent over the live well and used his ballpoint pen to raise the lid and check for bait. About two dozen dead shrimp and a few small menhaden floated on the surface of the water. Three fishing poles were in their holders attached to the sidewalls of the boat. Shark checked the small storage bin. Inside were a couple of bottles of sunscreen, a small screwdriver, a box of fuses, a pack of cheese crackers, and a small package of tissues. No fishing license or wallet, which he'd hoped for, but a business card from the Westin for Gus Manley, Accountant.

Next, he turned the key and checked the fuel gauge. It was still half-full. He tried the engine, and it caught immediately. He turned off the powerful twin Kawasakis, then knelt down to study the blood stains more closely. There was one large stain about the size of a salad plate and multiple small stains that appeared to be splatter. The stains were dry, and Shark couldn't help but think how difficult it was going to be to remove them after they had been baked on by the sun. He couldn't tell if they were human or animal.

Dell popped up out of the cabin. "Nothing much in there except what one would expect: Life preservers, signal gun, flare, sleeping bag, enough food for a couple of days. What about the blood? Can you tell if it's human?"

"No."

"So what do you think? Is this a crime scene?"

Shark paused for a moment. "Too soon to tell. If the blood is human, then probably. If not, then we may just have a fisherman who fell overboard or is off with a friend in another boat. There's a business card for someone who works at the Westin in the accounting department. Isn't that where Stephanie Grimes works?"

Dell nodded her head. "Yep. Think this is his boat?"

"Don't know yet. But it sure seems like people around Stephanie Grimes are dying or disappearing."

"Interesting. So do we haul the boat to shore or leave it here?"

"No, we definitely have to tow it in and let the team go over it. If the owner comes back and finds his boat gone, then I'm sure he'll call to report it stolen."

Dell felt sweat run down between her breasts. The waistband of her khakis couldn't have been any wetter if she'd just pulled them out of the washer. "Then let's get this show on the road before we die from heat stroke," she said as she stepped back into the Marine Patrol boat.

Russ threw Shark a towline, and he secured it tightly to the Grady. Once Shark was back aboard the patrol boat, he gratefully accepted the bottle of water Dell handed him.

"Think we should alert the Coast Guard? Have them make a couple of passes overhead and see if they spot anybody?" Dell asked.

"I hate to when we don't even know if anyone's missing yet, but I think we'd better err on the side of caution and have them do a couple of fly-bys."

"Yeah, can't you just see Miss Crime Beat reporter—what's her name, Rebecca something—splashing the fact we failed to contact them all over the front page?" Dell asked.

"Sands."

"What?"

"Sands. That was her last name."

"How come you remember that?"

"Don't know, just do."

Dell stared at him for a moment. "Did you pay a little closer attention to her than you want to admit?"

"No! You know how I feel about the press."

"Yeah, but she was a looker."

"I didn't notice," Shark said, then drained his bottle of water.

Dell rolled her eyes. "How come when some women walk into a room, men immediately start salivating? Then when the rest of us walk in, no one pays any attention to us?"

"I think it has to do with pheromones," Russ called over his shoulder.

"What the hell is a pheromone?" Dell asked.

"They're chemicals secreted by the body that attract the opposite sex. They're supposed to be odorless but stimulate something in the brain," Russ said.

Shark nodded. "I read an article about that once. It said researchers sprayed a chair in a waiting room with the male pheromone and more women sat in that chair than any other in the room. Also, they sprayed some on a couple of pay phones and more women used them."

Dell chuckled. "Well then, maybe you better buy some of that chemical and douse yourself in it, Shark. Maybe you could find you a mate that way."

Shark gave her the finger.

Chapter Eight

Rebecca was excited as she sat down at her desk at *The Island Packet* and began to pound out her story on Art Grimes. She'd scored pay dirt in Spartanburg. She learned about the trial, his DUIs, the arrest on the charge of molesting a neighbor child, and the fact that he had a gambling problem. Whether or not that had anything to do with his murder was yet to be determined. Her job was to throw it all out there and see what floated to the top.

She'd been surprised to learn from Art's brother, Stan, that Art's daughter lived on the island, and his son in Savannah. She'd called Stephanie Grimes several times but hadn't been able to reach her. She would track her down tomorrow. She was still trying to locate a phone number or address for the brother.

She finished typing her story and filed it so it would make the morning paper then leaned back in her chair, exhausted. Rebecca glanced at her watch. She couldn't believe it was ten-thirty. When she'd called to cancel dinner on the way to Spartanburg, she'd promised Hunter she would come by later, but she was just too tired. Her stomach started making strange noises, and she realized she hadn't eaten since her Whopper about noon. She grabbed her cell phone and decided to call Hunter on the way home. Even though she was starved, she couldn't stand the thought of more fast food. She would fix some scrambled eggs as soon as she took a quick shower. Rebecca waited until she was almost home before she dialed Hunter's number. She wanted an excuse for not dropping by.

Shark didn't have much to say as he and Dell finally headed to Beaufort around 10 P.M. The owner of the Grady White had turned out to be Gus Manley. The only interesting thing they'd found after interviewing his boss was the fact that Stephanie Grimes had filed a complaint against him for sexual harassment. But the investigation had gone nowhere. Stephanie had stated in her complaint that Gus was constantly telling dirty jokes and "coming on to her." But no action had been taken against him. And he'd been out on sick leave for the past month.

The blood on the deck had not been human, fortunately. They'd learned from Gus's wife that he'd recently been diagnosed with epilepsy as a result of a head injury from an auto accident, and he'd been having seizures lately. His doctor had advised him not to go fishing alone or to drive until they could see how his new medication was working. Obviously Gus hadn't paid much attention, since his car was found in the parking lot at Schillings' Boat House, and the guys on the dock reported seeing him head out alone the morning before. The men hadn't been concerned since he frequently stayed out for a day or two at a time.

So their theory was that Gus may have had a seizure and fallen overboard. The Coast Guard had searched the area until dark and would resume the search in the morning. Once the word went out, many of Gus's fishing buddies had also shown up in their boats and begun to assist in the hunt. The worst part had been telling Gus's pregnant wife that he was missing.

Overall, it had been a long day. And they still hadn't reached Brent Grimes.

Shark heard Dell start to snore. He was just about to rag on her about falling asleep but decided to leave her alone. She'd looked exhausted all day and still wasn't eating much.

Shark thought more about the possibility of moving onto

a boat. He could avoid this almost hour-long drive twice a day on the most dangerous road in South Carolina. But he would miss times like this with Dell, driving back and forth together and sharing what was going on in their lives. He wanted to ask her if Jazz had said anything to Josh about their relationship. But he didn't think it was fair to put Dell in the middle.

If he moved onto a boat, would his and Dell's friendship retain its strong bond if they saw each other only at work and occasionally on weekends?

He pulled up in front of Dell's house on Lady's Island. Josh had left the porch light on for her.

Shark leaned over and gently shook her. "Dell, wake up. You're home."

"I'm not asleep," she muttered.

"Like hell. You were snoring."

"Shows how much you know. I don't snore."

"Says who?"

"Josh. He said I just purr."

Shark laughed. "Just get outta here."

Shark stopped at the convenience store and bought two more packs of cigarettes. As soon as he got home, he opened the refrigerator, pulled out a beer, and picked up the phone to call Jazz. She wasn't home. He left a message on her answering machine and asked her to call him no matter how late she got in. Then he headed for the shower.

Stephanie Grimes was finishing her bacon and eggs around 10:30 P.M. before heading out to work. She was almost done when Andrea entered the kitchen, rubbing her eyes.

"Sorry if I woke you up," Stephanie said as she ate the last of her toast.

"You didn't. Actually, the food smells good. Maybe I'll scramble a couple of eggs. I wanted to make sure you saw the note about the lady reporter calling several times."

Stephanie picked up her plate and rinsed it off in the sink. "Yeah, I saw it and threw it in the trash. I don't want to talk to her."

"She's not the only one who called, just the most persistent."

Stephanie wiped her hands on the dishtowel. "I don't have anything to say. Let the answering machine keep filtering the calls for a few days. Okay?"

"No problem. But you might want to think about giving them a statement. Then maybe they'd leave you alone." Andrea grabbed the skillet Stephanie had used, added some butter, then turned on the burner. "What are you going to do about your dad's funeral?"

"Nothing. I don't want anything to do with it, and neither does Brent."

"So you finally got hold of him?"

"Yeah, he's scuba diving down in Key West."

"But you can't just leave your father's body in the morgue or wherever he is."

"He's got a brother. I assume Uncle Stan is still alive. Let him deal with it. I've got to run, or I'll be late."

Andrea was relieved to see that Stephanie still didn't seem upset about her father's death. She'd wondered after it all sank in if that would be the case.

Andrea scrambled the eggs and sat down at the table. She sighed when she saw the three cassettes she still needed to type to deliver in the morning. Even though the nausea had abated, she was still struggling with the fatigue. About the time she'd be feeling better, it would be time for another treatment.

Chapter Nine

Shark pulled up in front of Dell's the next morning a little after eight. A couple of minutes later, she climbed in the passenger seat of the car and reached for her seat belt.

"You look awful," Shark said. "Bad night?"

"You could say that."

"What's the matter?"

Dell avoided his eyes and stared straight ahead. "If I tell you, you've got to promise not to tell anyone."

Noticing her glum expression, Shark said, "Hey, you're beginning to scare me a little here. What's going on? You and Josh having trouble?"

Dell took a deep breath then blurted out, "No, I'm pregnant."

"I knew it!" Shark said excitedly. He reached over and kissed her on the cheek. "That's wonderful! Just call me Uncle Shark. So why the long face?"

"We hadn't planned on this right now. I guess the antibiotics I was on for my tooth screwed up my birth control pills."

"What did Josh say?"

"Oh, he's ecstatic."

"So why aren't you?"

"I don't know. It just scares me. I come from such a dysfunctional family that I wasn't sure I ever wanted to have a kid."

Shark took her hand. "Hey, you'll make a wonderful mom. Just learn from all the mistakes your parents made. I envy you. I wish Laura and I'd had a child."

"Remember, you promised not to tell anyone. I don't want people to know until I get past the first trimester, in case something goes wrong."

"Nothing's going to go wrong. I think you should tell the sheriff."

"No way, he'd want to put me on desk duty, and there's no need for that—at least not yet. Let's get going, so we won't be late for work."

A few minutes later as they crossed the Lemon Island Bridge, Shark asked, "Has Josh seen Jazz lately?"

"I think they grabbed a quick burger last week when he was in Charleston. Why?"

"I don't know. It just seems that I talk to her answering machine more than I talk to her. And sometimes it takes her a day or two to get back to me. Did she say anything to him about us?"

"He didn't mention anything specific. Why don't you just marry the woman and get on with it?"

"Every time I bring it up, she says she's not ready yet."

Dell glanced in his direction. "She really hasn't been divorced that long."

"Yeah, but neither one of us is getting any younger. I thought women were all supposed to be worried about their ticking biological clocks."

"Maybe she doesn't plan on having any kids. Frankly, I don't know how she would fit them into her career."

Shark passed a logging truck. "But she says she wants at least two."

"Then you better figure out a way to waltz her down the aisle and get started."

"Got any suggestions?"

Dell thought for a moment. "I've got a great idea! Why not buy airline tickets to some exotic place like Bermuda or St. Croix and just show up at her place and whisk her away? You could get married while you're there. Some of those places you don't even have to have a blood test, and there's no waiting period. That way she wouldn't have the hassle of trying to plan a wedding or anything. Then you could just have a reception when you get back. What do you think?"

Shark glanced over at her. "You know, I kind of like that. But my luck, I'd appear at her door with the tickets, and she'd have to be in court the next day."

"Pick a holiday like Thanksgiving or something where there's a long weekend. That would give you four days."

"I'm liking this better all the time."

"Why don't I go online and check out which places you can get married without having to wait?"

"It wouldn't hurt to have the information."

Dell grinned and started humming "I'm Getting Married in the Morning."

"Hey, knock it off. Let's talk about what we need to do today."

"There's really nothing we can do on the Gus Manley case. Do you think they'll ever find his body?"

"Not if the sharks get to him first."

"Don't you think it's quite a coincidence that he worked with Stephanie Grimes? Do you think we should interview her again?"

"I agree that it seems kind of odd. But I don't really see any way she could be involved with his disappearance from the boat. So let's focus on the Grimes case. Maybe they'll release the body today."

Dell pulled a stick of chewing gum out of her purse. "I'll contact his daughter and see what arrangements she wants to make. I need to review Stephanie's and her father's phone records. Also, I'll check on his life insurance policy and see who the beneficiary is. Stephanie said her brother's on a dive trip to Key West so we can't interview him until he gets back. What about you?"

"I'm hoping the trace evidence report will be back. I'm toying with driving up to Spartanburg and talking with Grimes's neighbors and his former employer. See if I can find any friends or relatives who may be able to tell us more about his life. I dread the long drive, but I'm not sure I can get everything I need over the telephone. Wish his roommate would show up."

As they crossed the bridge onto the island, Dell asked, "Do you want to try and run all the prints we picked up from that bedroom and see if we get a hit?"

"Let's wait a day or two and see if he makes an appearance. If not, that's our next step."

Traffic was moving even slower than normal with all the out-of-state vehicles mingled in with the morning commuters who couldn't afford to live in the affluent community where they worked.

"Do you think Sheriff Grant will run for re-election?" Dell asked.

"I sure hope so, but I won't be surprised if he doesn't."

"Have you heard something?"

"Not really."

"At least he's a good boss. Who knows who we might end up with if he doesn't run."

Twenty minutes later, Dell sat down at her desk to start working on the Grimes case. Shark picked up the phone and called the Coast Guard to see if they'd found Gus's body. He'd just hung up the phone when Sheriff Grant walked in and threw a copy of *The Island Packet* on his desk.

"So Grimes had a gambling problem? Do you think there's a connection to his murder?"

From the look of confusion on Shark's face, Grant could tell he had no idea what he was talking about. "Don't tell me this reporter knows more about Grimes than you do!" He abruptly turned around and stormed out of the room.

Shark looked down at the newspaper, and Dell could see his ears turning beet red, a sure sign he was pissed, as he read something on the front page. He cursed under his breath and jumped up from his chair.

"What is it?" Dell asked, as she stood and hurried over to his desk.

"Sands." Shark shoved the newspaper at her, and Dell quickly read the article.

"What's the big deal? So we follow up on the gambling angle."

"She's interfering in our investigation. Don't you get it? She's trying to show us up."

"Aren't you overreacting a little bit here?"

"No. I'm going to go have a conversation with her. Coming?"

Dell shook her head. "I think I'll pass. I'm going to work on those phone records."

Shark stormed out of the room.

By the time he drove to *The Island Packet* office a few miles off the island, instead of cooling off a little, he was even angrier.

Inside the new two-story building, he flashed his badge to the receptionist and asked to speak to Rebecca Sands.

"Becca hasn't come in yet. Can I take a message?"

"It's important I speak to her right away. Can you give me her home phone number and address?"

The receptionist hesitated.

"Hey, it's not like I'm a serial killer or something. I'm a cop."

The receptionist flipped through the Rolodex on her desk, picked up a piece of paper, and wrote down the information.

"Thanks," Shark said.

As he hurried to the car, he saw her address was Westbury Park, which was only about ten minutes away. He grabbed his cell phone and dialed her number, but the line was busy. *At least I know she's there.* He decided to just show up at her door.

Shark pulled into the subdivision, a mixture of small Lowcountry houses mingled in with large three-story homes. Sidewalks lined the streets. Marketed as "the neighborhood you grew up in," it wasn't like any neighborhood he'd grown up in, that was for sure.

He drove around for almost ten minutes searching for her house number before he realized she must be in the apartment complex.

He parked, bounded up the steps, and found himself standing in front of her door: He wiped the sweat from his brow with his shirtsleeve and was embarrassed that the back of his shirt and his underarms were damp.

He reached out and jabbed the doorbell. When she didn't answer within ten seconds, he punched it again.

Suddenly, the door swung open. Rebecca held a cordless phone to her ear. Dressed in a white tank top and navy jogging shorts, she didn't seem surprised to see him.

"Hunter, I'm going to have to call you back."

Rebecca looked Shark up and down, liking the fact that he was secure enough as a man to wear a pink dress shirt with his khakis. Once she'd given Hunter a pink shirt, and he'd handed it back to her and said, "Only girls wear pink." She wondered what had caused the long scar on Shark's face.

"Something's come up," Rebecca said. "There's a cop at my door, and he doesn't look happy."

Shark tried to quell his growing anger.

Rebecca held up her finger to indicate it'd just be another minute. "No, there's no problem, just work related I'm sure. I'll see you for dinner tonight, I promise."

Rebecca disconnected then leaned against the doorframe, the action opening her top enough to give Shark a peek of creamy breast.

"What do you want?" she asked, a grin on her face.

"Aren't you going to invite me in?"

"And why should I do that?"

"So your neighbors don't hear the lecture you're about to get!"

"I guess you saw my article. Didn't you like it?"

Shark frowned. "I especially liked the part where you implied the detectives were inept."

"I didn't exactly say that." Rebecca turned and entered the kitchen, leaving the door wide open. Shark closed it and followed her.

"Want some coffee?" she asked as she picked up her cup off the counter.

"No thanks. Where did you get your information about Grimes's gambling debts?"

Rebecca grinned. "You know I can't reveal my sources."

"I don't think that would be considered privileged information," Shark said as he leaned against the kitchen counter.

Rebecca put her cup down, strode over, and stood right in front of him.

Shark noticed she didn't have on any makeup, and he could see small wrinkles starting at the corners of her eyes and mouth. He'd thought she was a lot younger the first time he saw her at the office but now realized she must be in her mid-to late thirties.

"I worked my tail off yesterday getting all that info, and unless you're willing to share with me as the investigation moves along, why should I help you?"

Shark tried to control his anger. "Did you forget I've already got a partner?"

"Shark," Rebecca said in a soft sexy voice. She looked up at him with smoky blue eyes. "We can help each other. I had a good relationship with the cops in Atlanta. Call them. They'll tell you I play fair."

Shark bristled and backed her up against the opposite counter. "Don't think that sexy act is going to have an effect on me. I don't work with anyone but Dell. And it'll be a cold day in hell before I ever cooperate with a reporter."

"We'll see," Rebecca said confidently.

"Why don't you just marry your rich boyfriend and give up this charade of being a working girl?"

"Why do you assume he's rich?"

Shark grabbed her hand and held it in front of her face. "Because he'd have to be to buy a rock like that."

Rebecca tore her hand away. "Not that it's any of your business, but he's a real estate agent."

"Probably one of those that sell enough to be included in the million dollar club every year."

When Rebecca didn't deny it, he knew he was right.

Rebecca moved toward the door. "I think it's time for you to go."

"Can't agree with you more. Just stay out of my investigation."

He was careful not to slam the door as he left. He didn't want to give her the satisfaction of knowing just how angry he was. He slipped his sunglasses back on as he exited the building. He wondered who her fiancé was. Then he remembered she'd called the person on the phone Hunter. He knew of only one realtor named Hunter and that was Hunter Cowan, who had to be at least ten years older than she was. His picture was always in the newspaper for something: Being a mentor at the school, donating money to the Volunteers In Medicine clinic, taking a bunch of kids from the Boys Club on a fishing trip on his huge boat. Shark felt that people who advertised their good works were doing it for what they got out of it, good publicity for their business. Why should he be surprised she would hook up with a guy like that? They deserved each other.

Once Shark was back in the car, he turned left onto Highway 278 instead of right, which would have taken him back toward the island. He punched in the office number on his cell phone. When Dell answered he asked, "Can you catch a ride after work back to Beaufort?"

"No problem. What's up?"

"I'm headed to Spartanburg."

Dell started laughing. "Guess your little meeting didn't go well."

Shark hung up on her.

Chapter Ten

Dell grabbed the stack of phone records of Art and Stephanie Grimes, relieved that Shark hadn't asked her to accompany him to Spartanburg, which was close to a four-hour drive.

Art had made multiple calls to his daughter's apartment and another number that turned out to be her cell phone. However, there were no calls from Stephanie's regular phone or cell to his house, which confirmed what she'd told them.

Dell tried to envision how Stephanie must have felt when her father suddenly tried to make contact after all those years. Her fear and anger had been apparent when they'd interviewed her. But enough to kill him or hire someone else to do it? No, she didn't think so. Which left them where? With the brother? Or maybe Shark would come up with some viable suspects today during his interviews.

Rebecca Sands entered the Sheriff's office to pick up the crime report for the previous twenty-four hours. She approached the desk and introduced herself to an elderly woman in civilian clothes.

Jeanette Wheeler looked up from the Michael Connelly book she was reading. "We normally fax that over to the paper. I didn't know *The Packet* had a crime reporter."

"They didn't until a few days ago. I'll be stopping in and

picking up the report each day, so you won't have to send it any longer."

Jeanette smiled at the young woman. "Whatever you say. You want me to get a copy for you now?"

"That would be great."

"Won't take a minute. Be right back."

Sergeant Red Tanner strode in the front door and immediately noticed the attractive young woman standing at the counter. Since the volunteer that worked the desk was absent, he asked, "Can I help you?"

Putting on a big smile, Rebecca introduced herself then continued, "So I'm still trying to learn my way around and get my feet wet. As I explained to the lady who was at the desk here, I'll be coming by each day to pick up the report."

"Not much big crime around here like you probably saw in Atlanta. Our biggest problem is theft. Not only from the rental houses and villas, but also from construction sites."

"Well, you did have a murder my first day on the job."

"Trust me, that only happens a few times a year."

Rebecca stepped a little closer to the officer. "I met Detective Morgan and his partner the other day. Can you tell me why everyone calls him Shark? Is he really that mean?"

Red smiled. "They call him that because he does a lot of shark fishing in his off time, and his boat is called Tiburon, which in Spanish means shark. He's a great guy."

Jeanette Wheeler walked up to the counter and held out a piece of paper. "Here you go, Miss Sands."

Rebecca smiled at the sergeant, then took the proffered paper. "Thanks so much for your help. I'll see you in the morning."

Tanner turned and watched her walk out the door.

"You can put your eyes back in your head now," Jeanette said as she sat back down at the desk.

"What do you mean?" Red said as he adjusted his equipment belt.

"You're too late. She's already got a big rock on her finger. I'm surprised it didn't blind you."

"I must have missed that," Red said as he headed toward

the locked door to the interior and punched some numbers into the keypad.

"That's because you were looking elsewhere."

Rebecca glanced at the paper and groaned. She could interview Gus Manley's family and write up a short article. At least that was a little more interesting than the wave of car smash-and-grabs and tools missing from construction sites. Couldn't they have some real crime around here? Shatter a drug ring, or uncover a murder-for-hire? She threw the paper disgustedly onto the passenger seat. She might as well go interview Stephanie Grimes.

As she pulled onto Pope Avenue, the skies opened up and heavy rain began to fall. Pop-up thundershowers were the norm this time of year. Unfortunately, it did nothing to squelch the oppressive heat, only made it more humid, if that was possible.

Rebecca wondered if Shark was on his way to Spartanburg. She grinned at the thought.

The rain had stopped by the time she stood in front of Stephanie Grimes's door fifteen minutes later. She rang the bell and watched as a pair of squirrels raced up the trunk of a tall pine tree. The rat-a-tat-tat of a woodpecker was close, but she couldn't locate him.

A petite redhead opened the door. "Can I help you?"

"Are you Stephanie Grimes?"

Stephanie hesitated before answering, "Yes."

Rebecca stuck out her hand. "Rebecca Sands. Can I have just a minute of your time?"

"Close the door," Andrea called from the kitchen. "You're letting all the cool air out."

Stephanie motioned for Rebecca to enter. "What's this about?" she asked as soon as she'd shut the door.

"What a lovely place you have." Rebecca walked into the kitchen and introduced herself to Andrea. She was surprised to see that big patches of her hair had fallen out.

"Who are you? What do you want?" Stephanie demanded.

"Do you mind if we sit down?" Rebecca asked.

"Yes, I do mind," Stephanie said, crossing her arms. Andrea stood up from her chair.

"I just wanted to offer my condolences about your father and ask you a couple of questions. I spoke to your Uncle Stan yesterday, and he asked that you notify him about the funeral arrangements."

"Who are you?" Andrea asked, since Stephanie seemed speechless.

"Someone who cares," Rebecca said softly.

"You're a reporter, aren't you?" Stephanie asked, trying to control her anger.

At this point, Rebecca decided honesty was all that was left. "Yes. I won't take much of your time. I just wanted to ask you a couple of questions about your father."

"I have nothing to say. Please leave."

"I know you hadn't seen your father since your mother's death. At least that's what your uncle said. Do you have any theories on who might have wanted your father dead? I checked, and you were at work when he was killed. I've also been trying to reach your brother, Brent. Do you have a phone number for him?"

"You sound like a cop instead of a reporter. We already talked to them," Andrea said.

Rebecca turned to Stephanie. "I'm a crime reporter at *The Island Packet.* I just moved here from Atlanta, and my first day on the job was the day your father was discovered murdered."

"I have nothing to say to you. Please leave."

Realizing she wasn't going to get what she'd come for, Rebecca said, "Again, I'm sorry for your loss. If you'd like to talk sometime in the future, here's my card." She dropped it onto the kitchen table, turned, and left the room.

Once she heard the front door close, Stephanie glanced over at Andrea. "I don't think this will ever end. What time's your doctor's appointment tomorrow?"

"At ten. It's just for blood work though. I don't have to see Dr. Bartholomeu for another week."

* * *

Rebecca rang the doorbell of Hunter's two-story, stucco, oceanfront home in Sea Pines Plantation. Although it was almost 7 P.M., the temperature was still in the nineties. She could hear the surf in the background as she leaned over and pinched a few dead blooms off the pink begonia in the large clay pot next to the front door.

"Come in, darling," Hunter said as he leaned over and kissed her cheek. "I told you not to bother ringing the bell."

Rebecca smiled up at him. His hair was completely white, which she'd found interesting in a man who was only forty-five. A genetic thing he'd told her. The first time she saw him across a crowded room, she'd thought he looked like Richard Gere.

"Sorry, I'm just not used to walking into a person's home unannounced."

"But soon, this will be your home too," he said as he closed the door.

Rebecca glanced around. The formal dining room on the right was a dark navy with white crown molding and contained a cherry table large enough to seat twelve. Opposite it was a formal living room, which she'd been in only twice.

"Let me get you a glass of wine," Hunter said as he took her elbow and escorted her down the hall and into the kitchen.

"Something smells good."

"Chicken Noel."

"What's that?" she asked as she accepted the glass of chardonnay.

"I just take some boneless chicken breasts and smother them in a sauce of cream of mushroom soup, sour cream, fresh mushrooms and white wine, then bake them for a little over an hour. I've made some rice, and I'm steaming some asparagus to go with it."

Rebecca's eyes were drawn to the mass of pans and utensils hanging over the island. She couldn't imagine what they were all used for. She owned three iron skillets ranging from small to massive and two saucepans. "Sounds wonderful.

You know I don't know how to cook anything that isn't fried, don't you?"

Hunter laughed.

"It's true. I cook just like my mama did. Fried chicken, chicken fried steak, fried cube steak and gravy, fried catfish."

"Then how do you keep this luscious body of yours so fit and trim?" he asked as he took the glass out of her hand, set it on the counter, and pulled her into his arms.

"Hard work. That's why I run every day and do kick boxing, which I can't find anywhere on this island."

Hunter leaned down and kissed her passionately. "After dinner, maybe I can figure out a way to give us both a good workout."

"A walk on the beach would be nice," Rebecca said coyly.

Hunter chuckled. "I had indoor gymnastics in mind."

He let her go and turned back to the stove. "I thought we would just eat here at the bar if that's okay with you."

"Absolutely."

Rebecca glanced over at the informal living room, which was opposite the kitchen. It was all really one big room. A fireplace constructed of irregular stones gave it a masculine touch. A red plaid couch and two matching chairs were grouped around the fireplace. A leather recliner stood opposite a flat screen television next to a wall of glass facing the ocean. It was too perfect. As if some decorator had come in and constructed one of those rooms you'd see in a magazine. Her place, on the other hand, was filled with treasures she'd unearthed at estate sales and second-hand stores—chests and tables she'd sweated over and refinished, old chairs she'd reupholstered. None of her cherished items would fit in here. Would *she*?

Hunter had wined and dined her from the first time they'd met, and she had no doubt that he loved her. He was kind to her, protective, and made her feel safe. But was that enough?

Rebecca gazed out at the sea oats moving slightly with the ocean breeze. A large boat with a yellow sail glided slowly through the water. Three small children played in the surf. A runner glanced at his watch as he pounded the sand.

"Earth to Becca. What are you thinking about?" Hunter asked as he fixed their plates.

"Nothing special. Just watching people on the beach."

"It won't be long before you can spend the whole day out there."

Her job was a sore topic between them since she'd arrived on the island. She loved working and couldn't envision not doing so. Hunter expected her to resign after they were married. It was the one thing they argued about. She'd been dependent on her first husband, Todd, a stockbroker, but she never intended to be in that position again. She glanced into the living room with its formal fireplace and furnishings and had trouble visualizing herself here. She wasn't sure how she was going to fit into Hunter's lifestyle. She'd grown up in a working class family. When she married Todd, he'd insisted that she give up her newspaper job, which at that point consisted of covering town council meetings and other boring assignments. Even so, she found she missed the chaos of the newspaper room. She could never get into shopping, meeting other wives from the brokerage firm for lunch, and other social events. She was more interested in getting inside the mind of a serial rapist, figuring out what made people get to the point where they would commit murder, and why mothers killed their children. She couldn't understand why other people weren't as fascinated with the criminal mind as she was.

She'd also hated being dependent on her husband for money. Todd had given her an "allowance" of a hundred dollars a week. And since she was home all the time, he'd been adamant about everything always being perfectly in place. She had even seen him run his finger over a shelf to check for dust. The marriage had lasted only a little over a year—the longest year of her life.

"Here we go," Hunter said as he set their plates on the counter and sat down on the barstool next to her.

"I saw your article in the newspaper this morning. Looks like your trip to Spartanburg was fruitful. Is that why the cops were at your door?" he asked.

Rebecca put her fork down. "This is yummy. Yeah, Shark Morgan, one of the detectives, was a little pissed. I don't know why. I offered to work with him, but he promptly escorted me out of his office. Then today, he comes begging for the information I uncovered."

"Did you share it with him?"

"Fat chance. Let him do his own digging if he's not willing to work together."

Hunter observed how animated Rebecca became when she talked about her work. "Maybe if you had, he might be more receptive to working together in the future."

"I doubt it. He's a stereotypical Southern cop who thinks a woman should stay home barefoot and pregnant."

Hunter reached for a piece of French bread. "But I thought you said yesterday that he had a female partner."

"That's right."

"Maybe you can work through her."

"I hope so."

Rebecca picked up her fork and took another bite. "So how was your day?"

"Crazy. My staff was going nuts. A tourist renting one of our houses in Palmetto Dunes Plantation found a dead roach in a closet and went bonkers. Another insisted we send someone over to clean the microwave in her rental house. A toilet overflowed in one of our villas here in Sea Pines. But I got a contract on a house in Wexford Plantation. Typical day."

"How do you put up with all that?"

"By relieving them of a lot of their money at the end of the week."

Once the dishes were stored in the dishwasher, they carried their coffee out to the screened porch.

The ocean breeze had picked up as the tide came in. Rebecca loved the sound of the pounding surf. The sky was painted with red and orange as the sun marched toward the horizon. A flock of seagulls glided effortlessly over the water.

"Have you decided on a date for the wedding?" Hunter asked.

"No, I'm just trying to get my feet on the ground and unpack my boxes."

"I don't understand why you insisted on getting an apartment when you could have moved in here. It would have been easier to unpack just one time."

"I know. But I want to be sure before we get married. After all, ours was a long distance relationship. You might find you don't like me as much when I'm around all the time."

Hunter set his coffee cup down on the table. "Come here, silly," he said, patting his lap. Rebecca hesitated for a moment, then sauntered over and straddled his legs facing him.

He smiled at her. "I'm not going to get tired of you. I love you. How many times do I have to tell you?"

"But you don't know how messy I can be. And I can't cook fancy things like you do."

Hunter ran his finger slowly down her arm. "So we'll hire someone to clean the house, and I'll do all the cooking if you want. Don't you know that none of that matters to me? I love you for you, not your domestic skills."

Rebecca smiled. "I know."

"I can understand why you want your own place until the wedding," he said reluctantly. "How long a lease did you have to sign?"

"Just six months."

"Then you better start thinking about where you want to get married and when. Six months isn't that much time to plan a wedding."

"I don't really want to have a big to-do. How about you?"

"I've lived here for over ten years, so I have a lot of friends and people I do business with I'll need to invite. Is that a problem?"

Rebecca hung her head. "I don't have a lot of money to spend on a fancy wedding. I thought we would just have something simple. Maybe just get married on the beach since neither of us is into the religion thing."

"Don't worry about the money. I'll pay for everything."

Rebecca shook her head. "That's nice of you to offer. But I want to pay for as much as I can."

Hunter lifted her chin and kissed her. "How serious were you about a walk on the beach?" he asked softly.

"Well, if you can figure out another way for me to work off that dinner, I might be willing to give up my beach walk."

Hunter grinned. "I think I can come up with something more stimulating."

Chapter Eleven

Shark pulled up in front of Dell's just before eight.

"You're late," she said as she fastened her seatbelt.

Shark yawned. "I didn't get home until almost one. You're lucky I'm here this early."

"So how did it go? Learn anything?"

Shark grabbed his travel mug of coffee out of the cup holder. Before he could reply, Dell held up her hand. "Wait, before you start, tell me about how it went with Rebecca Sands."

Shark frowned. "She's a pain in the ass. I don't know how they did things in Atlanta, but I sure as hell don't plan on working with her. She refused to give me any of the information she uncovered. I told her to stay out of our investigation."

Dell chuckled. "Oh, I bet that went over well. No wonder you had to drive all the way to Spartanburg. If you'd been nice, maybe she would have shared."

Shark yawned again. "She's got to learn up front that we don't do things the way they do in the big city. I don't want her bugging us all the time about whatever we happen to be investigating." Shark put his mug back in the holder and reached for his cigarettes.

"Don't even think about it," Dell said.

"Sorry, I'm still half asleep."

"So what did you find out yesterday?"

"I talked to Art Grimes's boss. Grimes wasn't very reliable, frequently late and often absent due to his drinking, but apparently did good work when he was sober. His boss said he hated to let him go but felt he had no choice. I talked to some of the other guys on the crew, but they said he mostly kept to himself. Didn't seem to know if he was into gambling or not."

"So who else did you talk to?"

"His neighbors and his brother."

"And?"

"Didn't get much from the neighbors. His brother said he was into sports gambling and would occasionally go to Atlantic City for the weekend. He didn't have any idea how much he might be in the hole for, but Art had tried to borrow a couple of thousand from him a few weeks ago."

"Did he know who his bookie was, or better yet his roommate's name?"

"Unfortunately, no."

"Did he say why he moved to Bluffton?"

Shark ran his hand over a rough patch on his cheek he'd missed when shaving. "He told his brother construction jobs were plentiful here, and he wanted to try and reestablish contact with his son and daughter since he was dying. Apparently, they opened him up and found that his pancreas was riddled with cancer, and it had already spread to other areas of the body. The doctors recommended chemotherapy and radiation but told him, even with the treatment, he probably had less than a year. So according to his brother, he decided not to go through it all and just live his remaining days the best he could. He didn't want to run up a bunch of debt and have the hospital try to collect from his kids. I got the impression his medical insurance wasn't that great."

"I can understand not wanting to go through all the treatments if they weren't going to help."

Shark turned onto Highway 278 and goosed it up to seventy. "His brother did say that if his daughter didn't want to handle the funeral arrangements to let him know, and he'd take care of it."

"They're supposed to finally release the body today. I'll

give Stephanie a call, but I won't be surprised if she doesn't want anything to do with it."

"Me either."

Dell took a sip of coffee. "I checked with Grimes's insurance company, and the fifty grand is split equally between his kids."

"That's not enough to kill somebody over."

Dell nodded her head. "I agree. I don't think Stephanie was involved. I wish her brother would get back so we could talk to him."

"When's he due in?" Shark asked.

"According to Stephanie, in a few days. She said he would contact us as soon as he returned."

Shark yawned. "Think the sheriff would bite on a quick trip to Key West to interview him?"

"In your dreams."

"Yeah, that's why I didn't bother to ask. Did you find out anything about the phone records?"

Dell filled him in as they crossed the bridge onto the island.

Andrea sat down in the chair in the laboratory at Dr. Bartholomeu's office. "Hey, Crystal, how you doing today?"

Crystal fastened the tourniquet tightly around Andrea's left arm and her plump black hand began searching for a vein. "More importantly, how are you doing?"

"Tired. I feel like I can hardly put one foot in front of the other."

"Your white count's probably low from the chemo. Make sure you avoid crowds and anyone with an upper respiratory infection or anything like that."

Crystal slid the needle expertly into Andrea's vein. Andrea made a face. No matter how often she was stuck, she still couldn't get used to it.

"How many treatments do you have left?" Crystal asked.

"Three."

"Well, hang in there."

"What all are you testing for today?"

Crystal wrote Andrea's name and the date on the tube of blood. "Dr. Bartholomeu ordered a complete blood count, platelets, and a human chorionic gonatropin test to see if the level has gone down any since you started this round of chemo."

"The HCG didn't decrease at all with the last round."

Crystal removed the cotton ball from the puncture site and taped a two-by-two gauze square in place. "I know. Maybe this time it'll work."

"I'm not holding my breath," Andrea said as she adjusted the scarf on her head.

"You've got to have a positive attitude. You should try mental imagery. Remember the electronic game, PacMan? Pretend an old PacMan is just eating up those cancer cells. Visualize your body as healthy when all this is over."

"I'll try."

"When do you see Doc again?"

"Next week."

"These results should be back in a couple of days if you want to call his nurse and find out about them," Crystal said as she washed her hands in preparation for the next patient.

Rebecca was just coming out of the sheriff's office when she ran into Shark and Dell.

"What are you doing here?" Shark asked gruffly.

"Just picking up the report for the last twenty-four hours."

"We always fax that over to the newspaper," Dell said.

"I'll be picking it up from now on." Rebecca wanted the staff to get so used to seeing her around they wouldn't watch what they said. If past experience proved correct, she'd be able to pick up bits and pieces from conversations going on around her. "Doesn't look like much the past twenty-four hours," she said waving the paper at Shark.

"Fortunately we don't have the amount of crime I'm sure you're used to seeing in Atlanta," Dell said.

"True. It was a rare day when there wasn't at least one murder. Shark, did you decide to make a trip to Spartanburg yesterday?" Rebecca asked.

Shark glowered at her. "None of your business," he said

as he pulled open the front door of the office and went inside.

Dell couldn't help but grin.

"I don't know how you stand to work with him," Rebecca said.

"Oh, he kinda grows on you."

"I doubt that." Rebecca turned and headed toward her car. Once inside, she adjusted the air conditioning and made sure her police scanner was on, not that she anticipated anything exciting happening on this fifteen-mile stretch of sand. She groaned when she thought about her next assignment interviewing the couple who'd be moving into the new Habitat for Humanity home in Bluffton that some guys from a church on the island had built. Even though she still liked to think of herself as the crime reporter, here she was, just another flunky assigned multiple mundane stories to cover.

Shark was shuffling papers on his desk when Dell walked in.

"You been talking to that reporter?" he asked.

"No, I went to the restroom."

"Oh."

"Why do you let her get to you like that?"

"What do you mean?" Shark asked, looking up at her.

"You two were shooting daggers at each other the whole time. Actually, it was kind of amusing. Like watching two kids playing king of the mountain."

"That's absurd." Shark searched his desk. "I don't see a report on the trace evidence. What gives? It should be back by now."

"I'll see what I can find out."

"Any word on Gus's body?" Shark asked.

"No, and they've called off the search."

"Crap."

Sheriff Grant stuck his head in the door. "Don't forget the meeting at one on emergency preparedness. We're going to discuss evacuation routes."

Shark groaned. "There's only one way off the island, so what's to discuss?"

"Just be there, both of you," Grant said as he disappeared down the hall.

Dell slipped her shoes off. "Let's hope we're as lucky this year as we were last. We didn't have to leave a single time."

"As long as we don't have to evacuate three times in a matter of weeks like we did a few years ago."

"And pray tourist season is over if we have to go."

Shark leaned his head back on the edge of his chair and closed his eyes. "I hate those meetings. It's all I can do to stay awake, especially after so little sleep. Will you poke me if I start to nod off?"

"Not if the sheriff's watching. I suggest you take a strong cup of coffee with you."

"A lot of help you are."

Dell reached for the phone and made two quick calls. "They're going to release the body today, and Stephanie wants nothing to do with making the arrangements. So I'll let you contact his brother since you're the one who met with him."

"Okay, but I want to call about the trace evidence first."

Shark's phone rang. He picked it up and listened for a minute then said, "I'll be right out." He turned to Dell. "Grimes's roommate finally showed up."

Shark escorted Trent Osbourne to their office. "This is my partner, Dell Hassler. Have a seat." He motioned for the middle-aged man to sit in his desk chair. Shark grabbed a folding chair from behind the door and opened it.

Dell noticed the man was perspiring profusely. "Would you like something to drink?"

Osbourne rang his fingers through a few strands of gray hair and tried to finger comb them across his balding head. "No thanks. I just want to get into the house and pack up my things."

"Of course, but first we have a few questions," Shark said. "Are you aware of what happened to Mr. Grimes?"

"Yes. I pulled in the driveway about nine last night and saw the crime scene tape. I went next door, and the neighbor told me about the murder. I was shocked. So I rented a room at The Hampton Inn for the night. I had an early morning appointment but came here as soon as I finished."

"What kind of work do you do?" Shark asked.

"I cover South Carolina and Georgia for a dental supply company."

"And you rented a room from Art Grimes?"

"Yes, I usually stayed there one or two nights a week."

"How well did you know him?" Dell asked.

Osbourne pulled out his handkerchief and wiped his brow. "Not well at all. He was usually three sheets to the wind by the time I got there, and I'd leave early the next morning."

"Did you know about his illness?" Shark asked.

"I knew he was sick occasionally, but he never confided what the problem was."

Dell leaned forward in her chair. "Do you know anything about his gambling?"

"Sometimes when he'd be watching a game on TV he'd start cussing and say he'd just lost a bundle. Of course I wasn't sure if that was a few dollars or a few hundred."

"Anyone ever hassle him about gambling debts?" Shark asked.

"Not while I was there, and he never mentioned anything."

"Do you know if he had contact with his daughter who lives here on the island or with his son in Savannah?" Dell asked.

Osbourne shrugged his shoulders. "I heard him on the phone a couple of times begging someone to listen to him, but I don't know who he was talking to."

"Did he ever have any visitors while you were there?" Shark asked.

"One time I came in, and he had some woman there. She stayed the night. I got the impression the next morning that he'd picked her up in a bar."

Dell leaned back in her chair. "Do you know anything about his friends?"

"Sorry, I can't help you. Like I said, I was just there long enough to catch a few hours sleep. We weren't buddies."

"And can you tell us where you were when he was murdered?" Shark asked.

"When did he die?"

"Two nights ago about three A.M.," Shark answered.

Trent thought for a moment. "I would have been at the Holiday Inn in Vidalia, Georgia. I should have the receipt here," he said as he opened his briefcase.

Shark cleared his throat. "Just one more question, Mr. Osbourne. Did you and Mr. Grimes have any kind of sexual relationship?"

Osbourne's mouth dropped open. "What? Of course not!"

"I didn't mean to offend you, it's just something I had to ask."

Once they ascertained that Trent Osbourne had nothing more to offer, Shark followed him to Art Grimes's residence and watched as he removed his belongings.

Chapter Twelve

"I'm going to see if I can catch a little more sleep before I have to go in. Will you make sure I get up by ten?" Stephanie asked as she leaned against Andrea's bedroom door.

Andrea picked up her teacup. "Sure."

"Are you feeling okay? You look a little peaked, and it seems like you've got something on your mind."

"Just tired, and I've been thinking about my treatment again in a few days."

Stephanie yawned. "Just keep telling yourself they're almost over."

"I know. I'm just depressed since my hair is almost gone. Going to have to start wearing the wig in another day or two."

Stephanie crossed the room, leaned over, and gave her a hug. "Maybe soon you'll be able to throw that old thing away. I feel like the new medications are going to make you better this time."

"I hope," Andrea said softly as tears welled up in her eyes.

Once Stephanie closed her bedroom door, Andrea carried her teacup to the bathroom. As she removed the scarf from her head, large clumps of hair came with it. She stared into the mirror. Tears spilled onto her cheeks. She looked away, picked up the can of gel she used to shave her legs, and squirted some into her palm. She rubbed it over her scalp then picked up the razor.

A little after twelve, Marissa Langford disembarked from the plane at Savannah International Airport. She was unaware of the middle-aged woman who followed a few paces behind.

Marissa made her way downstairs to the Hertz counter to finish the paperwork for the Mercedes she'd reserved and to claim her baggage. She couldn't believe she was back at the same airport from which she'd fled not that long ago.

A few minutes later she stepped outside, and in the short length of time it took to load her bags and the painting of Shark, she was hot and clammy. She'd forgotten how unforgiving August was in the Lowcountry.

She jumped into the car and buckled up. She had an appointment in two hours with her attorney, James Kellum, to prepare for the hearing on Monday. Kellum had assured her that she had nothing to worry about, that he was convinced the judge would rule in her favor on Marcus's will. As soon as the hearing was over and the taxes paid, he was prepared to wire the balance to her account in Paris or wherever she desired.

Exiting the airport, Marissa wasn't surprised by the heavy traffic. Ever since the book, *Midnight in the Garden of Good and Evil*, tourist season had brought a flock of people to Savannah. Add those scurrying to the beaches, golf courses, and tennis courts on Hilton Head Island and it made for one big traffic jam.

She'd reserved a room at the Rhett House Inn, one of the finest bed-and-breakfasts in downtown Beaufort. The old plantation home, built in 1820, had been restored to its former splendor.

She wondered what it would be like to see Shark again. In her haste to leave the island after Marcus's murder, she'd been so busy placing the house with a realtor and clearing up his affairs, she hadn't seen Shark to say good-bye.

He'd called her once to thank her for the Wyland sculpture she'd sent him, and until she'd phoned him from Paris a few days ago, they'd had no further contact.

As Marissa passed the Sun City retirement development and approached the turn to Highway 278 for Hilton Head Island, many of the cars in front of her put on their signals. She had no desire to revisit the place islanders called "their little piece of paradise." It held nothing but bad memories for her.

She was pleasantly surprised to see the old road to Beaufort was being replaced with a new four-lane. A plethora of businesses and developments had sprung up along the entire route. At the rate the developers were taking over, all the tall pines and marshland would soon be gone.

Marissa glanced at her watch, pleased to see she'd have time to check in and unload the car before her appointment.

Monique LaBlanc wasn't concerned that she'd lost sight of Marissa. She knew where she was headed—she had a reservation at the same bed-and-breakfast.

On the drive to Beaufort, she enjoyed the rich leather of the interior and all the bells and whistles of the Lexus SUV, far more luxurious than anything she'd ever been in. She'd figured Ears would rent her an old jalopy, as tight as he was. Must be some rich client footing the bill. This was the second time a job had taken her to the United States, but her first time on the East Coast.

The scenery was fascinating. She'd never seen such tall pine and oak trees. At times, they covered the road like a canopy. She'd been surprised to see what she had always considered swamp land advertised on FOR SALE signs as "marsh" land. And it looked as if they paid a premium price for it.

In some places, small, run-down houses butted up against new developments. Large, gated housing areas announced themselves as plantations. A variety of businesses lined the road to Beaufort, from a beer distributor to a place that sold golf carts.

Once she reached Beaufort and located the Rhett House Inn, she was stunned. It looked like something out of *Gone With the Wind.* She admired the white three-story home with black hurricane shutters, stately columns, and wide verandas. Rocking chairs graced the porch, and a hammock was suspended between two of the columns. Several white ceiling fans attempted to cool those resting on the porch. She was going to enjoy this assignment.

She entered the small parking lot at the rear and saw Marissa unloading her bags. Monique waited until Marissa disappeared through the rear entrance before climbing out of the car. She grabbed her bag and admired the small vegetable garden and an array of blooming flowers as she hurried toward the back door.

Marissa finished filling out the check-in form and was waiting for the proprietor to get her key when an overweight, middle-aged woman stepped up behind her.

"Can you believe this heat?" Marissa asked.

The woman set her bag down and pushed her glasses up on her nose. "Reminds me a touch of South Africa."

"Really? I've never been there. Do you travel a lot?" Marissa asked.

"Oh, I manage a couple of trips a year."

Marissa had trouble placing her accent. "Where are you from?"

The woman hesitated for a moment. "Originally from Scotland, but I've spent the last ten years in Australia."

"What brings you to Beaufort?" Marissa asked.

"An old school chum invited me over for a few days. Never been in this part of the country so I thought, why not?"

The proprietor returned and handed Marissa her key. "Room one hundred and one. If you need anything, just let us know. Would you like help with your bag?"

"Thanks, but I can get it," Marissa said as she took the key and grabbed the handle of her suitcase. She turned to the woman she'd been speaking with. "Enjoy your stay."

* * *

It was a little after six when Shark turned onto his street and saw an unfamiliar black Mercedes parked in front of his house. He pulled into his driveway and was surprised to see a woman placing a package next to his front door.

She turned as he shut off the engine and stepped out of the car. "Shark, hello."

"My God, Marissa? Is that really you? I hardly recognized you with short hair."

Marissa reached up and ran a hand through her bangs. "Yeah, it's me."

"So when did you get into town?" he asked as he unlocked the front door.

"This afternoon. I had a short meeting with my attorney and decided to drop this off on my way back to the Rhett House."

Shark stared at the package in her hand. "Well, come on in."

The first thing Marissa saw when she stepped inside was the Wyland sculpture that had been her husband's and that she'd shipped to Shark when she put everything up for sale. "Looks like you've given this a good home."

Shark nodded. "I've sure enjoyed it. But remember, I said you could have it back whenever you wanted."

"No, it's yours. You appreciate it much more than I ever would."

"Come on in the kitchen, and I'll get us something to drink."

"I hope this isn't an inconvenient time to stop by. Don't let me interfere with any plans you have for this evening."

Shark motioned for her to have a seat at the kitchen table and pulled out a pitcher of iced tea. "I was just gonna take the boat out for a little while and try to get cooled off. Interested in going for a spin?"

"Did you ever buy that big fishing boat you always talked about?"

Shark chuckled, set a glass down in front of her, and joined her at the table. "On a cop's salary, not hardly. I've still got the same old Sea Pro."

Marissa picked up her glass and took a long drink. "Sweet tea is about the only thing I've missed from here."

Shark grabbed his heart and feigned an attack. "Oh, how you wound me."

Marissa laughed. "Sorry. That didn't come out the way I meant."

"Yeah, I hear ya. I'm sure you had better things to think about than an old cop in Beaufort."

"That's not true. I can't tell you how often I've thought of that time we went fishing. I was so desperate to get out of the house after Marcus's funeral and then spreading his ashes."

"I was floored when I called you that day just to see how you were doing and suddenly found myself blurting out the invitation to join me—and you accepted!"

Marissa smiled. "It was such an awful time. I would have gone anywhere anyone suggested to get out of that house. You were a lifesaver. And later when you handed me a fishing pole and told me to reel in the fish, I was scared to death I would do something wrong."

"You did fine."

Marissa wrinkled her nose. "Until you cut it open and started pulling the guts out. I thought I was going to be sick."

Shark laughed. "Well, you hid your discomfort well. So are you game for another fishing lesson?"

Marissa paused for a moment. She could go back and sit in her room alone or go with Shark. "Sure, why not."

"Let me change clothes, and I'll throw some things in a cooler and grab some bait. What's in the package?"

"Just a little something for you."

Marissa handed it to him. Shark ripped off the brown paper and was shocked to see a painting of himself fighting a fish on a rough sea. He was speechless for a moment, then noticed Marissa's name in the lower right hand corner. "You painted this?"

"Guilty."

"It's great! I'm impressed. I didn't realize you were an artist."

"I don't know if I qualify to call myself that, but I've enjoyed the classes I've been taking."

"This is really cool. Thanks." Shark propped the painting

up on the counter. "Do you want a glass of wine or a beer while I'm changing clothes?"

Marissa shook her head. "No, I'll wait until we're out on the boat. Anything I can do while you're changing?"

"If you want to grab the cooler out in the garage and put some beer and wine in it, we can pick up some sandwiches or a bucket of chicken on the way to the dock."

"I can handle that. Go change."

As Shark pulled some old clothes out of his dresser drawer, he wondered if taking Marissa out on his boat was going to cause a problem with Dell. Though Marissa had been cleared of the Hilton Head shooting, Dell was still convinced there was a cloud of suspicion around her and her past. Dell would not be happy when she found out about this evening. She'd think he was getting romantically involved with Marissa again. On the other hand, Dell was always telling him not to go fishing alone. He'd just enjoy catching up with Marissa and not worry about what his partner was going to say.

Forty-five minutes later Shark steered his boat through the maze of barges and equipment being used to build the new Broad River Bridge and checked the coordinates on his GPS until they were over one of his favorite fishing spots. He tossed the anchor overboard and, once it caught, tied the rope off to a cleat.

There was a slight breeze, and the sky was streaked with dark purple. Shark couldn't tell if the sun had slipped over the horizon. The tall trees on shore blocked his view.

"I'd forgotten how beautiful it is on the water at dusk," Marissa said as she leaned back and pulled her legs up under her.

"Yeah, I know what you mean. I've been thinking about selling my place and moving onto a boat."

"I'm surprised you didn't do it years ago as much as you enjoy being on the water."

"I guess I figured if I ever got around to getting married again that most women would prefer a house to a boat."

"That's probably true."

"Let me get a couple of lines in the water, then we can eat." Shark grabbed a knife out of the tackle box. He had a tangled line and didn't want to take the time to work out the knot.

"So what did your attorney think about Diane DeSilva's claim?"

Marissa pulled two beers out of the cooler and handed one to Shark.

"He thinks it's a bunch of bull. Marcus's will specifically stated if something happened to BJ I'd inherit his share."

Shark stored the tangled line in a plastic grocery bag, then attached a large gold hook to the line on the fishing pole. He baited both poles with menhaden, cast a line on each side of the boat, and placed the rods in PVC pipe he'd installed so he could sit back and have his hands free.

Shark grabbed his beer off the deck and sat down facing Marissa. "If I remember right, the will was pretty specific, so I doubt there'll be a problem." He ran his finger around the top of the can. "I can't believe you're really out here on the boat with me again."

Marissa laughed. "I don't believe it either. But I do miss being around the water."

Shark opened the cooler and handed her a submarine sandwich. "You said on the phone the other night you've been taking flying lessons?"

"Yes, and I love it. My uncle took me on a helicopter ride at the county fair when I was about five years old. Ever since then I've wanted to learn to fly."

As she talked about her new passion, Shark had an opportunity to observe her closely. She'd changed. Not just her hair, but something else about her. She was more relaxed, more sure of herself, as if she'd finally grown into her skin. Dressed in a pair of white slacks and a pink cotton blouse with the sleeves rolled up, she looked so different from the Marissa DeSilva he'd known, who always wore nothing but the best. He thought back to how infatuated he'd been with her as he investigated her husband's death and blushed at the thought of what a fool he'd made of himself.

Marissa handed Shark the bag of potato chips. "So tell me what's going on in your life. Got a woman friend?"

Shark grinned and nodded his head. "Actually I do. She's a lawyer in Charleston. We met right after you ran off to Spain."

From the look on Shark's face Marissa could tell he cared a lot for the lady. "Are you two going to get married?"

"One of these days I hope."

"So what are you waiting on?"

Shark balled up his napkin and placed it in the trash bag. "Actually, I've asked her, but she isn't ready yet. I don't want to push her and scare her off. She hasn't been divorced that long, and I think she's enjoying her independence. But Dell thinks I should just show up at her door and whisk her away to some Caribbean island to get married."

"You mean Dell approves? That's hard to believe."

"Well, she should. She's the one who introduced us. It's her sister-in-law."

"I get the picture now. Do you think she loves you?"

"She says she does, but our schedules are crazy. It's been almost three weeks since I've seen her. Either she's tied up with a court case, or I'm in the middle of an investigation."

"Think she'd move to Beaufort, or would you head up to Charleston?"

Shark crumpled his beer can. "I'd probably have to go up there. We haven't really talked about it."

"I agree with Dell. Run off and get married, then work out the details."

One of the fishing poles bent over slightly, and Shark could hear the line singing as something attempted to swim away. He could tell it was small, so he didn't hurry as he leaned over and picked up the pole out of its holder.

"You want to bring this in?"

Marissa laughed. "No thanks. I'll let you have all the fun."

Shark took his time reeling the line in, then he released a small stingray. He rebaited the hook and flung the line back into the water.

Marissa turned at the sound of an outboard motor. Shark saw the running lights of another boat approaching. The captain cut the engine about a quarter mile from them, off to the left. They heard the anchor splash into the water, then the familiar strains of "Margaritaville."

Shark looked at Marissa, and they both started laughing. "I still remember you singing your heart out to 'Cheeseburger in Paradise' that night you brought me home from the hospital, and I bribed you into staying all night," Marissa said.

"Which almost cost me my job," Shark said. "So what about you? Seeing anybody?"

Marissa shook her head. "No. I've had an occasional date, but I wanted to spend some time discovering who I really am. And after being divorced once and widowed twice within just a few years, I swore off men for a while."

"I guess that's understandable. I still can't believe you're really here," Shark said as he reached for another couple of beers.

"Sorry about not saying good-bye before I left. I fled as quickly as I could and never had any intention of returning. Too many unpleasant memories—but you're not one of them. You were really kind to me through that whole mess, and I don't think I could have gotten through it without you. Especially since your odious partner was ready to string me up to the nearest tree."

Shark chuckled. "Dell was convinced you were a black widow. She has a vivid imagination." Shark propped his feet on the cooler. "So anyway, tell me about Paris and Spain and all the places you've been since you left."

"Well, I had an unnerving experience in Paris recently."

"What was that?"

"I was standing next to someone who got shot."

Shark sat up a little straighter. "That's pretty scary. What happened?"

After Marissa finished telling him the story, Shark leaned over and grabbed the bag of potato chips. "Did they ever find out who shot the guy or why?"

"They hadn't by the time I left. They were still asking people who might have seen something to contact the police."

Shark picked up his beer bottle and clinked it to hers. "May Lady Luck continue to watch over you."

This woman is like a magnet for disaster. How many times

can you stand next to someone who is struck by lightning and not get hit?

Monique followed Marissa to her attorney's office and then to the subdivision where the cop lived. Ears had told her his name before she left Paris, and she'd spent the afternoon locating his address and becoming familiar with the area. Her wig was gone along with the padding in her clothes. Dressed in a pair of black jeans and a white silk shirt, she looked totally different.

She'd followed them to the boat dock and waited in the parking lot until they returned to shore. As they turned onto the street where the cop lived, she continued down the block and parked where she could see the entrance to the subdivision. A short time later, she followed Marissa back to the Rhett House.

Once Monique was back in her room, she placed a call to Ears and reported in. Ears informed her he would speak to their client and call her back with instructions.

Monique was flipping channels two hours later when her phone rang.

"Our client is not happy that Miss Langford contacted the cop as soon as she arrived. He's concerned that they spent several hours together. His instructions are that if the opportunity presents itself, you're to take her out. Understand?"

Monique was stunned. She'd signed on to follow someone, not kill them.

"Are you still there?" Ears asked.

"Yes."

"Any problem with that?"

"No, I guess not, but I'm traveling light. Don't have a lot of tools to work with."

"Do the best you can. Our client will make it worth your while."

Monique hung up and immediately pulled out her laptop and logged on. She wanted to see what poisonous plants were indigenous to South Carolina. She knew her chances of finding a source for a gun on the street were probably slim. She could buy a knife tomorrow, but she detested them. They were a little more up close and personal than she liked.

Chapter Thirteen

At 5:45 A.M. the phone shrilled on Shark's nightstand. He groaned as he rolled over and looked at the clock then fumbled for the phone in the dark. "Morgan." He listened for a moment then dialed Dell's number.

"Hello," she mumbled.

"We've got a hit-and-run on Highway 278 near Rose Hill Plantation. Pick you up in ten minutes."

"Crap," she uttered as she disconnected.

Shark hadn't even come to a dead stop before Dell, juggling two travel mugs of coffee, came racing down the steps. "Figured you wouldn't take time to brew a pot," she said as she handed him a mug. "Sorry, but it's decaf."

"Thanks, that's better than nothing." He placed the mug in the cup holder and turned the car around. Once they crossed the Broad River Bridge, Shark ran his hand over his chin. "You'd better give me that electric razor out of the glove compartment."

"I thought you were looking a little shaggy there."

"I didn't shave yesterday, and it was late when I got back from the boat last night, so I didn't bother."

"You should be careful going out by yourself like that, especially at night. Look what happened to Gus. They still haven't found his body."

Shark hesitated for a moment. Then before he lost his nerve, he blurted out, "I wasn't alone."

84

"So who'd you rope into going with you? Your neighbor, Gary?"

"No, Marissa Langford."

Dell gulped, then punched him on the arm. "You shouldn't say things like that when I have my mouth full. You're lucky you're not wearing this coffee. So how did Marissa end up on your boat?"

Shark filled her in on what had transpired the night before, including Marissa's close encounter with a bullet.

"I still think she and her ex-husband were in cahoots. I bet he was the one who took a pot shot at her."

"Do I have to listen to that black widow stuff again? Did you forget you never came up with any evidence at all to link them together after their divorce? And it certainly wasn't for lack of trying."

"So let me get this straight. She shows up with a painting she did of you, you invite her for a boat ride, and you two play catch-up. Please tell me you kept your pants zipped!"

"Dell!"

"Okay, I'm sorry. I guess that's your business. But I just know how out of control you were every time you caught a glimpse of her the last time around. And I'm still convinced she's involved in some kind of scheme with her ex."

"She's totally different. I hardly recognized her. And it was like catching up with an old friend. That old fire in the belly for her wasn't there."

"I believe that fire was a little lower than your belly. So how long is she here for?"

"She's heading back to Paris right after the hearing on Monday."

"Good! It can't be soon enough as far as I'm concerned. By the way, Jazz called last night. Said you two were fishing tomorrow."

Shark turned off the razor and handed it back to her. "Yeah, I'm finally going to get to see her. Three weeks seems like three months."

"Maybe if we can catch some breaks today and get done early, you could go on up this evening."

"I like the sound of that, but you just want to get me out of town to make sure I don't see Marissa again."

Dell looked at him and smiled.

A short time later Shark pulled the car into the grassy median of Highway 278 behind two patrol cars and the coroner's vehicle.

Officers directed traffic and tried to keep people from slowing to check out what was going on. Anna Connors was just off the side of the road kneeling over a body. Shark couldn't tell if their victim was male or female until he and Dell got closer. The young Hispanic man dressed in a black T-shirt and jeans looked as if he were asleep.

Shark pulled the camera out of his bag and began snapping pictures of the ground around the body. Dell combed the area placing pieces of glass from a headlight into small Ziplock baggies.

Connors stood up. "He was hit from the front and thrown about thirty feet. Probably died from internal injuries. Not a lot of noticeable head trauma since he landed on the grass. That could look different on autopsy. I recovered some flakes of silver paint. I bagged them for you already. From the position of impact I would say you may be looking for an SUV or a van—something that sits up high."

"Great. They're only the most popular vehicle on the road. What else can you tell me?" Shark asked.

"According to a pay stub in his pants pocket, his name is Tomas Sanchez."

"Driver's license?" Shark asked.

"No."

"Which means he's probably illegal."

"Looks like he may have been hitchhiking since he was hit in front," Dell said.

Connors nodded. "I agree."

"Who did he work for?" Shark asked.

"Four Amigos, the new one in Bluffton."

"I didn't know there was one out there. I love the one on the island," Dell said.

"The one in Bluffton hasn't been open very long," Anna said.

"What about tire tracks?" Shark asked.

Connors shook her head. "No skid marks and no tire prints. It didn't help that he was dressed in dark clothing. It appears that whoever ran over him didn't even slow down."

"Maybe the driver thought he hit an animal or something," Dell said.

Shark nodded. "Could be. There's a lot of deer out here. But you'd think if you hit something that big you'd stop to see what it was."

Rebecca Sands was on her way home from the convenience store in Bluffton where she'd gone to buy a newspaper and grab a Cafe Mocha from Starbucks when traffic suddenly slowed to about twenty miles per hour. Five minutes later, she saw two police cruisers and a couple of other vehicles parked in the median. She'd failed to grab her police scanner before she headed out, but she figured it was just another accident, a daily occurrence on the four-lane race track to I-95.

As the officer waved her by, she turned to see what was going on and caught a glimpse of Shark and Dell. If the detectives had been called, there had to be a body. Her pulse kicked up a notch as she put her blinker on, slowed down, and pulled off onto the grass. She grabbed her bag with her press ID, a couple of disposable cameras, and a pad and pen, then started jogging the couple of blocks back to the scene.

The officers were busy keeping traffic flowing, so no one challenged her. Shark, Dell, and another woman all had their backs turned blocking her view. Rebecca noticed a paramedic smoking a cigarette as he leaned up against the side of an ambulance. She pulled out her ID and approached him.

"Hi, Rebecca Sands. I'm a reporter with *The Packet*. What's going on?"

Daniel Banks ground his cigarette out with the toe of his Nike. "Haven't seen you around before," he said as he stared openly at her. "Name's Daniel." He extended his hand.

Rebecca quickly shook his hand. "I'm new. What's going on?"

"Hit and run."

"Victim still alive?"

"No."

"Male or female?"

"Male."

"Got a name?" Rebecca asked as she glanced over to make sure the detectives hadn't noticed her.

"Can't help you there. Hey, you want to get a drink some-time? I can show you around the island. Tell you all the tourist places to avoid and where the locals hang out."

"Thanks, but I don't think my fiancé would approve. Do you know what happened here? Got a description of the vehicle involved?"

Disappointed that he'd been shot down, Daniel leaned back against the ambulance and crossed his arms. "Not really. I'm just here to transport the body to Charleston for the autopsy."

"Who's the lady over there with Shark and Dell?"

"Anna Connors, the coroner."

"Oh, a lady coroner. That's a little different."

"She used to be a cop."

"That explains it. Well thanks for your help," Rebecca said as she jammed her notebook into her bag, pulled out a new camera, and moved slowly toward the victim.

Shark was bent over taking a picture of something in the grass, and Dell had a plastic bag open, ready to retrieve whatever it was. The coroner was facing away from Rebecca, making notes on a pad of paper. Rebecca steered clear of the detectives and crept up behind the coroner. Then she leaned to the right and snapped a picture of the body. At the sound of the click, Anna turned her head.

"Who are you?" Connors demanded.

Shark looked up and groaned. "She's a reporter from *The Packet*." He started toward her. "You can't take pictures here. Give me that camera."

Rebecca dropped the camera into her bag, turned around, and took off running. Startled, Shark handed his camera to Dell and started after her. One of the officers directing traffic saw Rebecca running from the scene with Shark in pursuit but couldn't cross traffic to assist.

Shark cursed at Rebecca as he ran. She had gotten a

jump-start on him, but it wasn't long before he'd closed the distance between them.

He grabbed her by the arm and swung her around. "What do you think you're doing?"

"My job!" she yelled at him.

"Give me the camera," he said, grabbing at her bag.

"No! You have no legal right to take it from me. Haven't you ever heard of freedom of the press?" She flailed at him.

Shark caught her from behind, pinned her arms to her side, and said, "I may not have a legal right, but I've got a moral one. You're not going to plaster that man's picture on the front page. You can make this easy or hard. Your choice, but I'm not letting you go until I have the camera."

Rebecca's right foot shot back in an attempt to kick Shark in the shin. He yanked her back towards him to get her off balance and leaned her against his chest, her arms still pinned to her side.

"You try to kick me again, and I'll arrest you for assault on a police officer," he said into her ear.

Realizing she was out-muscled, she tried another tactic. "Is this the only way you can get close to a woman?"

Shark didn't say anything for a moment, then whispered. "Trust me, I have no desire to get close to you."

Rebecca turned her head just enough to look at Shark's face and could tell he was angry. "Okay, truce. I'll trade you information for the camera. Just tell me the victim's name and what you know, and I'll give you the camera."

"I'm not giving you anything, and I don't think you're in much of a bargaining position," Shark said without loosening his grip.

"That's silly. I'll have a report shortly anyway. So you might as well barter while you can. A hit-and-run, right? What kind of car are you looking for? Maybe I can help."

Shark was seething, but she had a point about knowing everything shortly anyway. "That's our assumption. That's all you're gonna get. Now give me the camera."

"Tell me his name, and the camera is yours," Rebecca whispered seductively as she gazed up at Shark, his mouth just inches from hers.

Shark stared down at her. "You're the biggest pain in the ass I've come across lately. Why don't you just go back to the big city and do us both a favor?"

"Sorry. You might as well get used to having me around. I'm going to be here a long time. Now, his name, and you get the camera."

"Tomas Sanchez. Now give it to me."

"Let go of my arm first. You're hurting me."

"Do you promise not to run?"

"Yes, I promise."

Shark cautiously let go but kept his hand a few inches from her arm. Rebecca rummaged in her bag, pulled out the camera, and gave it to him.

"Thank you. Now stay out of my way and don't pull a stunt like that again."

"Yes sir," Rebecca said as she fired off a salute.

As soon as Shark turned around and stomped away, Rebecca ran to her car. She didn't want to be around when Shark discovered she'd given him a camera filled with the trip to Charleston she and Hunter had made a few days before.

As soon as she pulled out onto Highway 278, she started laughing.

Chapter Fourteen

Andrea was still in bed when Stephanie arrived home from work and looked in on her a little after 7 A.M. She wasn't surprised to see that Andrea had shaved her head. Last time she'd lost her hair they'd found it everywhere: in their food, on the couch, in the shower. Maybe it would be easier this way. She just prayed the chemo would work this time. She didn't want to admit it, but she was afraid it wouldn't. And she couldn't imagine her life without Andrea. The bonds they'd formed went beyond friendship. They were family. Both damaged in some way, they drew strength from each other to keep going.

She'd begun to bargain with God. Promising to go back to church—a place she hadn't entered since her mother died—do some volunteer work, or something. She was getting desperate. Andrea appeared weaker every day. Even more disturbing, she seemed to be giving up. But could she blame her? Would she have been able to survive all that Andrea had been through?

Stephanie made her way quietly to the kitchen and pulled the makings for a grilled cheese sandwich out of the refrigerator. As she waited for the skillet to heat up, she placed a mug of water into the microwave and grabbed the box of mint tea bags. She was tired. Tired of worrying if the cops would find out she'd lied to them, if Brent was somehow involved in her father's death, of the stress of Andrea's illness, and of thinking about being alone if Andrea died. She didn't have any other close friends or a man in her life. Was she destined to spend the rest of her days without a husband and family? Why did life seem so easy for some and so hard for people like her?

Once they finished at the crime scene, Shark and Dell headed to Four Amigos in Bluffton.

The restaurant wasn't open yet, and there was no answer when they knocked on the front door. They hurried around back and found the kitchen door unlocked. Shark told the Hispanic man who was chopping onions he needed to speak to the owner.

"Not here," the man said, avoiding his eyes as he placed some fresh cilantro on his chopping board.

Shark pulled out his badge. "We need to talk to him immediately. Can you give me his phone number or address?"

The man turned pale. He laid the knife on the counter and looked right and left as if about to flee.

Dell raised her hands. "We mean you no harm. We just need to talk to your boss about one of his employees. If you'll give us his phone number or tell us where we can find him, we'll leave. Understand?"

"*Sí.*"

The man whipped a cell phone out of his pocket and punched in several numbers. A few seconds later he launched into rapid Spanish as his eyes kept darting back and forth between the detectives. Dell caught an occasional word she recognized, but couldn't really follow the flow of the conversation, which lasted a couple of minutes.

The man placed the phone back in his pants pocket. "Be here ten minutes. Wait in car." He picked up the knife and attacked the cilantro.

"Thank you," Shark said, as he turned toward the door.

"By the way, do you know what time Tomas Sanchez left last night?" Dell asked.

The knife paused in mid-air for a moment, but the man did not look up. "Not know Tomas Sanchez."

Not getting anywhere, the detectives went outside and leaned against the car. "Bet you ten bucks he doesn't have a green card," Dell said.

"I thought he was going to piss his pants when he saw my badge."

"I expected him to make a mad dash out the door. It must be terrible to live in fear of being deported."

Shark nodded. "Then they should enter legally. I bet if we checked the construction sites and landscaping services around here, at least half of the employees wouldn't be able to produce a green card."

"You're probably right."

A dark blue van pulled into the parking lot. The driver's door opened and a tall, thin, middle-aged Hispanic man walked toward them.

"I'm Felipe, the manager. What can I do for you, officers?"

"Does Tomas Sanchez work for you?"

"Yes. Is he in some kind of trouble?"

"He was killed last night by a hit-and-run driver on Highway 278, close to Rose Hill Plantation."

Felipe closed his eyes and expelled a long breath. "I'm sorry. He was a good man."

"Do you know where he lives or anything about his family?" Dell asked.

"He shares a house with six other men in Hardeeville. His wife and two kids are back in Mexico. Wait here and I'll get you the address where he stays."

As soon as he entered the restaurant, Dell said, "I'm impressed with the way he speaks English. Think he grew up in the States?"

"Possibly. I wish they'd all learn the language. Make it a lot easier dealing with them."

"Sanchez was probably trying to save enough money to bring his wife and kids here. Can you imagine sharing a house with six other guys?"

"No, I can't. I've seen some of those places they stay. I was in one tiny two-bedroom house that was falling down, and there were eleven men staying there, sleeping on cots."

Felipe returned and handed Shark a slip of paper. "That's the address he gave when he started working here about four months ago. I don't know if it's current. The men have a tendency to move around a lot."

"Do you know what time he got off work last night?"

"Around eleven."

"Did he normally hitchhike to and from work?" Dell asked.

"No, he usually drove an old red pickup truck. He mentioned a couple of days ago that it wouldn't start. Normally he'd have been able to catch a ride with one of his roommates who works here, but that guy's back in Mexico visiting his family."

"Do you know the names of any of the other men he stays with or where they work?"

"No, I don't. Sorry."

Shark handed him a business card and pen. "I think that's all for now. Would you write your full name and telephone number on the back here in case we have more questions?"

"Sure." As Felipe wrote he said, "I suggest you take someone with you who speaks Spanish when you interview his roommates. I doubt many of them speak English."

"We'll be sure and do that. Thanks for your help," Shark said as he stuck out his hand.

Felipe shook his hand. "If you can get me his family's address in Mexico, I'll forward a money order in the amount due him and a little extra."

"I'll make sure we get that information to you," Shark said.

As soon as they were in the car, Dell radioed in and asked who was on duty that was fluent in Spanish. The dispatcher informed her that Miguel Fuentes was and patched her through to him. She explained the situation to Miguel, and he agreed to meet them in the parking lot of the Wal-Mart Supercenter a few miles from Hardeeville.

Rebecca Sands raced home and took a two-minute shower, quickly blew her hair dry, and dressed in a pair of white slacks, a red button-down shirt, and a pair of white sandals. Seventeen minutes had elapsed by the time she was back in the car. She'd taken long enough to check the phone books for Hilton Head, Beaufort, Hardeeville and Ridgeland, but had found no number for Tomas Sanchez.

As she pulled out onto Highway 278, she hoped she could get back to the scene before the detectives left. She figured the first place they'd go would be to the victim's home to notify next of kin. Her hope was to follow them then interview the family when they left. Once that was accomplished, she'd get the picture developed then go to the office and write her story.

When she arrived back at the scene, the ambulance was loading the body, and Shark and Dell were standing next to the coroner's car talking with Connors. Rebecca drove on past, down to the red light at the entrance to Rose Hill Plantation. She pulled over to the side of the road and watched her rear view mirror.

A couple of minutes later, Shark and Dell entered their vehicle. Shark did a U-turn and headed in Rebecca's direction. She was afraid he'd recognize her car if she remained parked along the side of the road, so she signaled then pulled out onto the highway. She drove slowly, figuring Shark would be in the passing lane as he headed to his destination.

She turned her head as he roared past, hung back a little, and followed them until they turned onto Highway 46 toward Bluffton.

She kept three cars between them and continued on straight when they turned right. She saw the sign for the Mexican restaurant and figured that was their destination. She slowed at the four-way stop then pulled into the Nickel Pumper's parking lot and turned around. She drove past where the detectives had turned off then pulled into a hardware store parking lot a block up the street.

While she was waiting, she called the office and asked one of the other reporters to run a Google search on Tomas Sanchez. The only thing that came up was a Cuban painter by that name and a site about his family genealogy.

Thirty minutes later, she saw Shark's car race past. She let two cars get between them before she pulled out.

She followed them north on Highway 278 past the scene of the crime. Ten minutes later, she was surprised when Shark made a right turn into the Wal-Mart Supercenter. She continued on. *Now what? I can't pull over to the side of the road because he'll see me for sure, and there's nothing between here and the gas stations up at I-95. Why is he going to the Wal-Mart? Need some bullets for his gun or something? He must be meeting someone, but who?*

Rebecca proceeded down the road and a couple of minutes later pulled into the gas station and parked so that her car was facing the road. She only hoped the detectives didn't double back and head to Beaufort or Savannah or who knew where in between, or she would be screwed. She didn't know the area that well yet.

Suddenly Shark's car, followed by a patrol car, drove past. She let one car get between them then took up the chase again.

A block later, at the T-road, they turned left and headed toward Hardeeville. She hung back, hoping she wouldn't draw their attention.

The detectives led her to a small neighborhood with run-down homes. She drove on past as they pulled up in front of a small brown house with three old pickup trucks in the driveway. She grinned when she saw the Hispanic officer. *Of course, they probably need a translator, dummy.*

Rebecca drove back to the convenience store she'd passed, used the restroom, and refilled her mug with some French vanilla cappuccino. Back in the car, she tasted it tentatively. Totally different from Starbucks, but not bad.

She returned to the south side and parked down the street from the police cars. She picked up her pad and wrote down the main questions she wanted to ask then tried to compose them in Spanish. She'd spent her junior year of high school in Ecuador as an exchange student. The dialects would be different, but maybe she'd be able to wade through.

Chapter Fifteen

When they returned to the office, Shark began to call local garages to see if anyone had brought in a silver SUV with a broken headlight and front end damage, while Dell elicited Miguel Fuentes's help in contacting their victim's family in Mexico.

They worked through the morning without much success. When Miguel was called out on another assist, he assured Dell he would continue to try to get in touch with the Sanchez family.

After Miguel left, Dell glanced down at her watch. It was only eleven-thirty, but she was ravenous. "How about we break for lunch? I'm starved."

"Might as well. I'm not getting anywhere with the garages. If a tourist hit our victim, we may never find him. Especially if he waits until he gets back to Ohio or wherever to get his car fixed. What do you have in mind for lunch?"

"Why don't we walk over to Just Pasta? I love their food."

Shark stuffed some papers into a folder and laid it aside. "That's fine with me. I've never had a bad meal there, and it can't hurt to introduce the little bambino to Italian food early."

"Shhh, keep your voice down."

After Shark dropped Dell off at home a little after six, he kept thinking of what she'd said about driving up to

Charleston that evening. He was aching to see Jazz and wasn't sure he could wait until the next day. Even though he was tired, he reached for his cell phone. He hit speed dial for her office number, but the voice mail picked up, so he hung up without leaving a message. No answer at her home number, and her machine kept beeping then disconnecting. As a last resort, he tried her cell phone but got a recording saying the number was not in service. Surprised, he hung up.

Shark dragged his weary body through the front door and entered the living room, collapsing onto the couch. His eyes were drawn to a small cactus plant on the coffee table. The soil was so dry it was cracked, and the plant was almost petrified. Fearing if he stayed on the couch, he'd fall asleep, he picked up the pot, slowly made his way to the kitchen, and threw it into the trash. He flipped on the small TV, so the silence wasn't so apparent, and pulled his last beer out of the fridge.

As he sat at the kitchen table, half watching the national news, he tried to decide what to do about Jazz. He didn't want to show up without calling first, but the thought of trying to figure out something for dinner and spending the evening alone again just wasn't appealing. He decided to take a quick shower and change then try to call her again.

A half-hour later, he came out of the bedroom dressed in jeans and a long-sleeved blue cotton shirt. He set a small duffle bag by the front door, quickly entered the kitchen, and tried her home number again. Still no answer. He grabbed his keys and decided he would try her from the road.

As he closed the front door, he remembered his Mustang was in the garage getting some brake work done. He wasn't supposed to take his unmarked police car out of the county, so he hurried over to the old pickup truck he hauled his boat with and climbed inside.

It was a little over an hour before he reached the outskirts of Charleston. Excited at the thought of seeing Jazz, he decided to stop and buy a couple of bottles of her favorite wine, Rutherford Hill Fume Blanc, and a twelve pack of beer for their fishing trip scheduled for the following day.

When he came out of the liquor store, he tried her number again, and since it was busy this time, he knew she was home. Relieved, he began to sing "American Pie" as he made his way to northern Charleston. It wasn't long before he pulled up across the street from Jazz's villa.

As Shark reached over to grab the wine and his duffle, he saw Jazz, dressed in a sexy red cocktail dress, come out of the complex on the arm of a tall man in a gray suit that probably cost more than Shark's monthly mortgage payment. The man helped Jazz into a dark green Jaguar. Shark felt as if he'd been sucker-punched. He scrunched down in his seat so Jazz wouldn't see him, even though she seemed oblivious to anyone but her companion. Shark saw Jazz laughing as they pulled away.

As the Jaguar pulled out, Shark waited a few seconds then swung out into traffic. He wasn't worried about losing the Jag. He was a good tail man. He could stick to a vehicle like cotton candy to a three-year-old's hand. He felt sick at the thought that Jazz was seeing someone else. Was the guy in the car the reason she seemed to change the subject every time he mentioned getting married? How long had they been seeing each other? Was he the reason she always seemed too busy to get together? Did she love this man?

Shark followed them all the way to High Cotton, a fancy restaurant downtown on East Bay Street. He watched as they entered and was pleased to see they were seated next to one of the front windows. Shark drove down Cumberland Street, found a space in the parking garage, and grabbed his Atlanta Braves ball cap. He pulled it low to hide his face and hurried to a restaurant directly across the street from the one Jazz and loverboy had entered. He pulled open the door of Slightly North of Broad, commonly referred to as SNOB by the locals, and stepped inside.

The restaurant was one large room. The kitchen was at the rear and in full view of the dining room, nestled under a brick arch. From the look of the interior and the fancy bar on the right side of the room, it appeared to be a high-end place.

"One for dinner?" the hostess asked.

"Yes, and I'd like a seat by the window please."

He accepted the menu and ordered a Corona after his waitress rattled off the nightly specials.

Shark opened the menu and groaned when he saw the main courses and their prices. Grilled barbecue tuna $20, roast leg of lamb, a mere $26.50. Hadn't they ever heard of a burger and fries?

When his server brought his beer, he bit the bullet and ordered a small ribeye. He'd contemplated getting just a couple of appetizers, but they'd added up to almost as much as the dinner.

Over the next two hours, he nursed two Coronas and ate the delicious food very slowly, while watching the interplay between Jazz and her friend.

They talked their way through drinks and a four-course dinner. They didn't hold hands or touch each other a lot, but Jazz laughed and seemed to be having a good time. When their dessert and coffee arrived, Shark settled his tab and returned to his truck. He moved it to a parking space where he could see the front door of the restaurant.

Forty-five minutes later they exited, Jazz's hand in the crook of the man's arm. They meandered down the street, stopping to look in a couple of shop windows. Romeo bought her a pink rose from a street vendor. Two blocks from the restaurant, they entered the Vendue Inn. He and Jazz had listened to some good music there a few months before in The Library, the inn's lounge.

Shark drove to the Harris Teeter grocery store a few blocks away and bought two sodas, two packs of cigarettes, and a cheap lighter. With Dell's pregnancy and Jazz detesting his smoking, he'd been trying to quit again. It'd been three days.

He drove back to the inn and parked down the street where he had a good view of the front door.

He ripped the cellophane off the pack of Marlboros and lit up. He savored the first wave of nicotine. As he sat alone, like on so many other stakeouts, his thoughts returned to his and Jazz's time together since Dell had introduced them. He remembered that Christmas day a couple of years ago when his partner had failed to tell him Josh's sister would be joining them. Initially he'd been a little upset, but by the end of the evening, he'd invited Jazz to spend the night in his guest room to give the lovebirds some privacy. Josh planned to propose to Dell that evening. He smiled as he recalled how they'd talked all night. In less than twenty-four hours, Jazz had completely captivated him. Afraid he would never find anyone that would make him happy again after Laura died, he'd been surprised at how much he enjoyed Jazz's company and how compatible they seemed. But as he thought back over their time together, he realized he was the only one that ever brought up the subject of marriage. And when he did, she always seemed to have some excuse about why they should wait. Maybe she didn't love him the way he loved her. Perhaps the guy across the street with his fancy clothes and car was the reason. Could he really expect a beautiful, professional woman to fall in love with a broke, road-weary cop? Maybe she considered him nothing more than a fishing companion.

Shark drained his soda and reached for another cigarette. It was amazing how easily one could fall back into old habits.

A little before one, Jazz's friend emerged from the club and hurried down the block. A few minutes later he returned in the Jag, parked in front of the inn, and beeped his horn.

Jazz emerged a little unsteadily. Romeo jumped out of the car and helped her into the passenger seat then roared off.

Shark followed them back to her place and watched as the man escorted her up the steps of the complex. Shark wondered if he would be staying the night. If so, he would have his answer.

Shark parked down the street and opened the other soda. His thoughts turned to Jazz in the arms of another man. Someone else holding her close and inhaling her scent. Would she take him to her bed?

Shark was lost in his thoughts and didn't realize the man had emerged until the Jag started up suddenly.

Shark smiled as Romeo's car disappeared down the street. Well, she wasn't sleeping with him, at least not tonight. After the Jag pulled away, Shark thought about knocking on Jazz's door and demanding an explanation but decided he would rather ask her about her evening and see if she lied to him. Plus, it looked like she'd had a lot to drink. He wanted her to have a clear head when they spoke.

Shark mulled over the idea of renting a room for the remainder of the night but decided instead to drive down to the dock and sack out in the truck. It wouldn't be the first time he'd slept in it, and he could use the men's room in the morning to shave and wash up.

Twenty minutes later, Shark relieved himself in some bushes at the dock then climbed back inside his truck and lay down on the seat. He punched his duffle bag a couple of times, trying to shape it into a pillow. He left the window open on the driver's side and hung his feet out. It was the only way he could stretch out.

Sleep was elusive. He feared that all of his dreams of a future with Jazz would be shattered in a matter of a few hours. If so, would he find himself falling back into the blue funk of depression that was as familiar as an old friend?

Chapter Sixteen

Rebecca Sands could hardly keep her car on the road as she yawned and made her way home about 10 P.M. She'd spent the day covering a function sponsored by the Historical Society in Bluffton then raced to Beaufort for a demonstration at the outdoor range and training ground for the Sheriff's Office. The department had coordinated an exhibition for their most recent graduating class from the Citizens' Police Academy.

She'd been surprised by the amount of high tech toys the department had accumulated through federal grants, and was absolutely amazed by the mock demonstration of a hostage rescue by the SWAT team. They'd used live ammo, and their commander had played the part of the hostage. Another member of the team, who was hidden in some tall grass, drilled one of the mock bad guys with a head shot from one hundred and four yards away. She'd been impressed. She knew of some large city departments that were not equipped half as well.

But being out in the glaring sun and killer humidity had taken its toll. She'd called Hunter earlier and explained she had developed a screaming migraine from the sun and begged off from dinner. She just wanted to get home, run the thermostat on her air conditioning down to about sixty-five, and soak in a lavender-scented tub.

It had been a long day. And she wasn't sure she'd made

the right decision not to use the photo of the hit-and-run guy from this morning. She'd been surprised the picture had come out as well as it had, but she just couldn't see plastering the poor man's face across the front page. She had lied to her editor—never a good thing to do—that she'd been caught by surprise and didn't have a camera with her. She wondered if Shark had developed the film he'd taken from her, and if so, if he would give her the pictures she and Hunter had taken on their trip to Charleston.

As she entered her apartment, the flashing red light on the answering machine caught her attention. She punched the button and wasn't surprised to hear Hunter's voice asking her to call him when she got in.

She kicked off her shoes, pulled the bottle of Limon rum from the cabinet over the sink, grabbed a Coke out of the refrigerator, and headed for the bathroom.

Rebecca lost track of time as she enjoyed two stiff drinks and luxuriated in the tub. By the time she toweled herself dry, she was practically asleep, and all she could think about was falling into bed. She knew Hunter would be upset if she didn't return his call, but she didn't feel like talking to anyone at the moment. She would give him a ring in the morning.

As she drifted off to sleep, she remembered Shark holding her close that morning, and how shocked she'd been that she liked it.

Monique LeBlanc slipped out of the inn around 6 A.M. She was on the hunt. Her research had revealed that multiple poisonous plants grew in the Lowcountry. Monique glanced down at the papers in her hand. She'd printed off the descriptions and pictures of some of the most common. Many were houseplants or used in flower gardens. She thought she had the best chance of finding an oleander, castor bean, or deadly nightshade plant. All were highly toxic. She was also on the lookout for a mushroom known as dead man's hand, or devil's snuffbox.

She'd successfully used poisons twice in the past. She preferred them to guns and knives. Many offered the opportunity to be far away by the time the first fatal symptom appeared.

Invariably, doctors began testing for bacterial infections when the patient showed up with nausea, abdominal pain, and bloody diarrhea. Few even considered poisons at that point. By the time the patient slipped into a coma and the kidneys shut down, frequently the family would request no autopsy be done. If the person had any history of health problems, most physicians acquiesced. According to an ex-cop she knew, many people got away with poisonings until the third or fourth time they used the same method on spouses or family members.

Monique watched two squirrels tentatively cross the street. The morning was pleasant, not too hot yet. She'd driven by a park down by the water yesterday and that was her destination. She thought she might have a good chance of finding one of the plants on her list there.

She stopped at Firehouse Books & Espresso Bar and bought a mocha latte and a muffin then headed toward the park.

Marissa was bored. She'd spent the day browsing through the shops in downtown Beaufort. She'd bought a couple of books at the Bay Street Trading Company and found a shady spot on a bench along the riverfront. But it wasn't long before the heat had driven her back to the air conditioning of the inn. She had the whole weekend ahead of her before the hearing Monday morning.

She thought about calling Shark and inviting him to dinner. She remembered him mentioning he was going to see his lady friend this weekend, so maybe she shouldn't. She hoped it worked out for him. Some men did okay alone, but he seemed to need a woman in his life. And he'd mentioned again how much he'd like to have a family.

She glanced at her watch. It was almost time for dinner. She decided to have a glass of wine on the veranda while she was waiting.

She made her way to the living room and poured a glass

of Merlot. As she stepped out onto the porch, she saw the middle-aged woman who had checked in the same time she had, looking at a brochure about the inn. Marissa sat down in the rocking chair next to her.

Monique looked over and smiled.

"I'm Marissa Langford. I don't think I caught your name the other day."

"Everyone calls me Babs, because they say I babble on all the time." She waved the brochure in her hand. "It says here that some big-name movie stars have stayed in this inn. Robert Redford, Nick Nolte, Barbra Streisand, and several others. I love Barbra Streisand. Did you know that the movie *Prince of Tides* was filmed around here?"

"No, I didn't."

"I've never stayed anywhere like this before. You don't find too many old plantation houses in Europe and Australia."

"I'm sure that's true."

Monique laid the brochure on the table. "Have you visited here before?"

"Yes, a few times. I lived briefly on Hilton Head Island, which is just a few miles from here."

"Back visiting friends?"

"No. I had to come back to settle my late husband's estate. The county courthouse is here in Beaufort."

"I'm sorry. You look too young to be a widow."

Attempting to change the subject, Marissa said, "I'm surprised to see you here. I figured you'd be spending all your time with your school chum."

"We spent the morning together, but her mother became ill this afternoon, and she had to take her to the hospital."

"How terrible. I hope it's nothing serious." Marissa motioned to the other brochure on the table. "According to the lady at the front desk when I checked in, the carriage tour is supposed to be nice. She said it was a great way to learn the history of the area, but she recommended doing it early in the morning due to the heat."

"I'll keep that in mind, but I haven't decided for sure yet.

What else is there to do around here since it seems I may be spending most of my time alone?"

"Charleston is only about an hour away. I'm thinking of heading up there tomorrow to do a little shopping at the old slave market. Then there's Hilton Head Island, about forty-five minutes from here."

Monique drained her wine glass. "I'm going to get a refill. Can I bring you one?"

Marissa saw that her glass was still half-full. "No thanks. I'm fine."

Monique entered the living room and refilled her glass with cabernet. She looked around to make sure she wasn't being observed, then pulled a small vial out of her pocket. She'd discovered several oleander plants on her walk this morning and had spent the afternoon drying and grinding a few of the leaves to a fine powder. A common ornamental plant in the South, few people realized how poisonous it was. She sprinkled a little of the powder into a clean glass and filled it with the cabernet, which she knew had more of an aftertaste than a merlot. She swirled it around to dissolve the powder. According to her research, the oleander had a bitter taste, but she was hoping the wine would mask it.

She went back out on the verandah and handed Marissa the glass. "Thought I would save you a trip and bring you a refill. This looks like a nice cabernet."

Surprised, Marissa accepted the glass and set it on the table. "Thanks."

"With this heat I figured the less we moved around, the better. You'd better drink up, or this old woman is going to get ahead of you."

An elderly gentleman dressed in khakis and a navy polo shirt wiped his brow with his handkerchief as he climbed the stairs to the porch. "Boy, this heat is something else. Mind if I join you?"

"Please do," Marissa said.

The man dropped into a rocker. "Name's Hank Barrows from Dayton, Ohio."

"I'm Marissa, and this is Babs."

"Nice to meet you. Where are you all from?"

Marissa ran her finger around the rim of her wine glass. "I've spent the last year in Paris."

"Lucky you," Hank said. "How about you, Babs?"

"Sydney, Australia."

Marissa motioned to the glass of wine on the table. "Care for something to drink? Babs brought another glass out for me, and I'm still working on this one."

"Maybe in a minute. Although I think something cold might fit the bill better."

"I know what you mean," Marissa said.

They continued to chat for a few minutes, and Hank decided to go inside and find some ice water and cool off in the air conditioning.

Marissa drained her wine glass.

Babs leaned over and picked up the fresh glass off the table. Noticing a little sediment on the top, she swirled it around a little. "I kind of like this cabernet. See what you think."

Marissa would have preferred a glass of iced tea. Most cabernets were too strong for her taste. However, she didn't want to appear rude. "Thank you," she said as she accepted the glass from Babs.

Babs watched as she held the wine up and looked at its color, fearful she would notice the sediment in the bottom. "Drink up," Babs said as she raised her glass.

Suddenly, a wasp appeared out of nowhere and began buzzing around Marissa. She shook her head trying to shoo it away, but the pesky thing lit on her bangs. She instinctively reached up with her right hand to send it on its way, and the wine glass slipped from her hand crashing onto the verandah.

"Oh my gosh. Look what a mess I've made," Marissa said as she stood and hurried into the house to find something to clean it up with.

Babs rolled her eyes and leaned her head back against the rocker. She'd come so close.

Chapter Seventeen

Shark slept fitfully, unable to find a comfortable position. Too many thoughts about Jazz and their future—or lack thereof—raced through his mind. At six o'clock, he went in search of caffeine and a restroom.

After a bacon, egg, and cheese biscuit and two large cups of coffee, he felt a little more human. Returning to the dock, he hurried to the men's room, shaved, and washed up.

He sat down on the top of the picnic table, took a sip of coffee, and watched as the forklift removed Jazz's thirty-foot Grady White from storage. The attendant gassed it up then the forklift delivered it gently into the water.

He grabbed the wine and beer from his truck and made his way down the ramp to the floating dock. The sky was overcast, and there was a chill in the air. The radio had said only a thirty percent chance of rain, but from the looks of the sky, he wouldn't be surprised if they got a shower or two. Shark unsnapped the canvas cover and stowed it in the cabin then checked the oil, started the engines, and let them run for a couple of minutes. He filled the live well with water then strolled up to the tackle shop where he bought ice and bait.

As Jazz walked down the ramp a little before eight, she smiled when she saw Shark already on the boat readying their fishing poles, and she picked up her pace.

His back was to her as she approached the boat.

"Hey, good-looking, need a first mate?"

Shark turned and smiled, "Only if they know a thing or two about fishing."

Jazz handed him the picnic basket she was carrying then stepped down into the boat. "You must have left at the crack of dawn. I figured I'd beat you here." She wrapped her arms around him and gave him a big hug. "It's so good to see you."

"I was tossing and turning all night, so I figured I might as well get on the road." Shark stared into her dark brown eyes, searching for signs of deceit. "I've missed you," he said as he lowered his mouth to hers. He intended to keep the kiss brief, but as his lips met hers, his need for her overwhelmed him.

Jazz eventually broke off the kiss. Looking up at him she whispered, "Wow! You sure know how to wake a girl up first thing in the morning."

"I'd like to wake you up like that every morning."

Jazz chuckled. "If you did, I'd never make it to work on time." She extricated herself from his arms. "Let's get bait and ice and get out of here so we can have some privacy."

"I've already taken care of that."

"Then let me put some of this food in the cooler, and we'll get underway."

Jazz fired up the two powerful outboards while Shark handled their lines, then she slowly threaded her way through the throng of boats and the no wake zone out into open water. There was little conversation over the roar of the engines as they made their way to one of her favorite fishing holes just off James Island.

Forty-five minutes later, they had baited lines in the water and sat down to enjoy a cup of coffee from the thermos Jazz had brought. The wind had picked up, and Jazz pulled up the collar on her jacket. "It seems like forever since I've seen you. I've got so much to tell you."

"It's been too long."

"I know what you mean, but it seemed like every time we

planned to get together, something either came up with the trial, or you were working on a case."

"So how's the trial going?"

"Good. That piece of scum child molester will be put away for a very long time."

They talked a little more about work, then Shark casually said, "I tried to call you several times last night. Did you get tied up at work?"

Jazz reached for the thermos and refilled their coffee mugs. "I'm sorry I missed your calls. An old law school buddy is in town and invited me to have dinner with him."

"Law school buddy?"

"Yeah, Miles and I used to be in the same study group in school. I hadn't seen him in a couple of years and was surprised when he called yesterday. He works at the Justice Department."

Shark began to relax a little. "So what'd you guys do?"

"Went out to dinner and talked about old times, and I caught up on what some of our former classmates are doing."

"Just dinner?"

Jazz frowned, but answered, "No, Miles wanted to go to a club, so we hung out at The Library for a couple of hours. Why all the questions?"

Shark smiled. "Just curious, that's all."

"Hey, you're talking to a prosecutor here. I know when I'm getting the third degree. What gives?"

Shark looked away, not wanting to reveal that he'd followed her the previous night, fearful he'd end up losing her for being such a fool.

Jazz planted herself in his lap and began to chew on his earlobe. "Care to tell me what's going on?"

"Is this the way you interrogate all of your suspects? No wonder they all confess."

"Do I need to interrogate you?" she whispered, as she peppered his neck with butterfly kisses.

Shark groaned and pulled her head up until his lips found hers. He tried to lose his feeling of guilt in her velvety lips and to stop her questions. But she broke off the kiss, stared into his eyes, and asked, "Honey, what's the matter?"

Shark paused for a moment then said, "Jasmine Delacourt, you know how much I love you."

"Then why do I have a feeling there's a 'but' coming?"

Shark stared into her eyes trying to muster his courage. "Because I screwed up royally. I tried to call you at the office last night a little after six. I thought I'd drive up, and we could start our weekend early. I also tried to get you at home, but your machine cut me off after a bunch of beeps. I even called your cell phone, but it said it wasn't in service."

"The battery was dead."

Shark took a deep breath. He knew it was now or never. "So I decided to drive on up and surprise you. I'd just pulled up in front of your building when I saw you and Miles get into his car."

"So why didn't you holler at me or something?"

Shark hung his head. "I don't know. Anyway, I followed you."

"You followed me?"

"Yes, to the restaurant and to the club," Shark whispered.

"I don't believe this," Jazz said as she jumped off his lap. "You're checking up on me? Don't you trust me?"

Shark stood up and reached for her, but she shrugged him off. "I do trust you. It's just that I was so shocked I didn't know anything else to do. My cop persona just took over."

"I don't think I like that part of you very much. So let me get this straight. You spied on us all evening. How could you?"

Shark ran his hand through his hair and paced on the deck. "Put yourself in my shoes. What would you have done?"

"Well, I wouldn't have jumped to conclusions like you did. But why didn't you just ring my doorbell after he dropped me off and ask me about it? Where did you spend the night?"

"In my truck, here at the dock."

Jazz moved away from him and hugged her arms close to

her body. She turned her back and didn't say anything for a minute. Shark moved over and stood behind her, careful not to touch her.

"I'm sorry," he whispered.

She turned and lashed out at him, "Shark, I don't need this. My ex-husband was into control. I promised myself after the divorce I wouldn't get into a relationship like that again. I never expected that kind of behavior from you."

Shark started to reach for her.

She backed away. "Don't touch me."

Shark could see his whole future disintegrating before his eyes. He had nothing left to lose. He reached over, grabbed her arm, and pulled her close. He could see tears threatening to spill from her eyes.

"Let me go."

"No. I won't let my stupid act destroy everything between us. I'm not controlling. That's not my nature. You have to admit that in all the time we've been together I've never exhibited any of those tendencies. I like the fact you're an independent woman. I love you, Jazz. Tell me, what would you have done if you'd chanced upon me with another woman?"

"I would have called out to you immediately. Or followed you to the restaurant and walked in and sat down beside you. But I would not have spent the whole evening spying on you. Why didn't you ask me about it right away this morning? Did you think I was going to lie to you?"

"I was hoping you wouldn't, and you didn't. I feel awful about following you. I know I blew it. Will you please forgive me? I promise it'll never happen again. Just tell me one thing. Is Miles single?"

Jazz tried to keep the stern look on her face and not smile, "No, he's married with a nine-month-old son."

Shark's face lit up.

"I think you were jealous, Morgan."

"You're damn right I was," he said pulling her closer. But she shrugged out of his arms and stepped to the other side of the boat.

"I need to tell you why Miles wanted to have dinner last night. As I said, he works for the Justice Department, and they have an opening. He offered me a job."

Shark's stomach did flip-flops. "In Washington?"

"Yes. It would be quite a career move."

"But what about us?"

"I haven't made a decision. I thought we should talk about it. There's nothing tying you here. How would you feel about making a move?"

Shark collapsed onto the large cooler and stared out across the water. "You know how I hate big cities. I can hardly stand Charleston, which isn't all that big. And I feel like I can't breathe if I get too far away from the water. I'm a small-town boy. What would happen if I resigned and moved up there with you, and then you didn't like the job or got a better offer someplace else?"

"I don't know. I can't guarantee anything. I just know it's hard to turn my back on an opportunity like this. Maybe I could try it out and see how it goes, and if it's going well after a few months, you could join me then. Anyway, it's not so far that you couldn't fly up and see me frequently."

Shark's head snapped up. "It sounds like you've already made up your mind."

Jazz shook her head. "No, honestly I haven't. I've just been playing different scenarios over in my mind since Miles mentioned it last night."

Shark could sense an air of anticipation and excitement in her body language and knew what her decision would be. In that instant he realized if she was willing to give up their future for her career, then she didn't love him as much as he loved her. He stood up and reached for her, then picked her up and started toward the steps down into the cabin.

"What are you doing?"

"Trying to convince you to stay right here and marry me."

Dell was aroused from a deep sleep by the smell of coffee and food emanating from the kitchen. She stretched and went to the bathroom. She walked back into the bedroom to find Josh standing there with a breakfast tray.

"Good morning. How about breakfast in bed for my lovely wife and mother of my child?"

Dell grinned and gave him a quick kiss. "How did you know I was famished?"

"Because all those books of yours on pregnancy say you have an insatiable appetite at this stage."

"Well, they're right about that," Dell said, jumping back into bed, and arranging her pillows against the headboard. "So what culinary delights do you have for me?"

"Orange juice, decaf coffee, toast, and an omelet with bacon and cheese, garnished with fresh fruit on the side."

"Oh my, I could get used to this."

Josh poured her coffee then returned for a tray of his own. Once they were snuggled in bed and enjoying their meal, he said, "So what color do you think I should paint the nursery?"

"Don't you think it's a little early to be thinking about that? We don't even know if it's a boy or a girl yet."

"It's a boy," Josh said emphatically.

Dell chuckled. "And how do you know that?"

Josh grinned. "I just do."

Dell picked up her glass of orange juice. "You just want it to be a boy."

"No, it wouldn't matter to me either way, but it's a boy."

"Well, I still think you better wait until they can determine the sex on a sonogram before you get out the paint. She might not like blue."

"So have you been thinking about names?" Josh asked, as he refilled her coffee cup.

"Not really. Why, have you?"

"Well, a little."

"And let me guess, Joshua Delacourt Jr?"

"And she wins the grand prize behind door number one!" Josh said, mimicking Monty Hall. "That's unless you don't like it."

"I had something a little more distinguished in mind, like Winston."

"Winston? Please say you're kidding."

Dell started laughing. "Yes, I'm kidding. I think Joshua Delacourt Jr. is a most distinguished sounding name."

"Good," Josh said, as he set both their trays on the floor. "I'm so glad you agree. Now how about a little loving for old papa here?"

Dell giggled. "Well I guess I don't have to worry about getting pregnant. Just think, in a few months we'll have a little one running around creating havoc. Does the thought of that bother you?"

"Bother me? No, I can't wait. Scare the hell out of me? Absolutely."

Chapter Eighteen

Sunday morning Rebecca, carrying a bag of bagels and lox, glanced at the black Porsche in Hunter's driveway and wondered who his guest was.

Hunter opened the front door, pulled her into his arms, and kissed her passionately. "I told you not to bother with ringing the bell, to just come on in."

Rebecca glanced at the car. "I wasn't sure who you might be entertaining."

Hunter led her by the arm over to the shiny automobile. "What do you think?"

"It's beautiful. Who's the lucky owner?"

A smile lit up Hunter's face. "You're looking at him."

Surprised, Rebecca asked, "But what happened to your Lexus? It was less than a year old."

"It was stolen Friday night."

"You're kidding. Did you report it?"

"Of course. But I figured it was probably halfway across the country by now, or in a chop shop, and when I saw this puppy, I couldn't resist. You know what they say about men and their toys. I'll take you for a spin after breakfast. Let's eat, I'm starved. I've made a pitcher of mimosas."

Over breakfast Hunter asked, "What do you think about flying to New York next weekend? I thought it would give you a chance to look at wedding dresses, and we could take in a couple of plays."

Rebecca pushed her plate away and leaned back in her chair. "You can't go with me to pick out a gown. I promise I'll run up to Atlanta or Charleston in a couple of weeks and see what I can find. I've gone online to David's Bridal and have an idea of what I want."

Hunter picked up his champagne glass. "I've started working on the guest list. You need to give me the names of the people you want to add, so I can get an idea of how large a place we'll need for the reception."

"There won't be that many. I just have a few friends from Atlanta I'd like to invite. What do you think about having the ceremony on the beach at sunset?"

"We'd have to get a permit from the town and set up a tent and chairs. Sounds like a lot of extra work to me. I had something more traditional in mind. But hey, we don't have to make a decision at the moment. Let's go take that spin."

Shark was in a lousy mood when he picked up Dell Monday morning. As Sunday had progressed, things had not gone well with Jazz. He was convinced she was going to take the job offer, and he didn't know how to stop her.

Dell handed Shark a brown bag filled with homemade chocolate chip cookies and buckled her seat belt.

"What's this?"

"Comfort food."

Shark concentrated on pulling into traffic. "You must have talked to Jazz."

"She called Josh last night and told him about the job offer. She said she wants you to go with her if she takes it. So what do you think?"

Shark stuck his hand in the bag and pulled out a cookie. "You know how I feel about Jazz, but I guess she doesn't feel as strongly about me. I don't see risking my career and moving to Washington with the possibility that, after a few months, she may decide to change jobs again. And you know how I hate big cities."

Dell's face lit up with a smile. "I'm sorry it's not working out with you two, but I'm selfish. I'm glad you're not going.

I'd hate to have to break in a new partner. Maybe she'll turn it down."

"I wouldn't bet on it. And I don't want to talk about it anymore. She has to make up her own mind."

"Will you be okay if she does go?"

"I'll survive."

"Well, just don't go getting mixed up with Marissa Langford again. I still can't believe she showed up at your house like that."

Shark glanced at Dell. "She'll be heading back to Paris today as soon as she gets out of court. And I told you, that old fire has gone out."

"Thank goodness. The thought of you two together would be more than I could stomach."

Shark chuckled. "And that wouldn't be good for a pregnant lady."

By the time the detectives had fought their way through the onslaught of traffic onto the island, Shark's mood had only gotten worse.

When he entered the office and found there was still no report on the trace evidence from the Grimes murder, he flew into a rage. "How do they expect us to solve this thing if we can't even get a report on what was found at the crime scene?"

"Cool your jets. Let me see if I can track down the report while you work on the list of silver SUVs that may have been involved in the hit-and-run."

Shark leaned his head against the back of his chair and looked up at the ceiling. "I swear two-thirds of all the cars on the road these days are silver. I'll try the garages and rental companies again, but I think I'm just spinning my wheels."

Dell could tell it was going to be a long day. She knew her partner was hurting at the thought of losing Jazz. Maybe she'd made a mistake introducing them. She'd been so sure as their relationship had progressed that it would lead to marriage, something she knew Shark desperately longed for.

She wondered how Shark would handle the rebuff if Jazz left. Dell recalled Shark's depression and destructive behavior after his wife died. It had almost destroyed their relationship as partners and friends. His drinking had gotten to the point that she questioned whether she could depend on him to cover her back in an emergency. She only hoped he was better equipped to handle the loss this time. Perhaps the baby would help. Or would it make him more aware of not having children of his own?

Traffic was barely moving, backed up for at least a half mile waiting to get through the stoplight in front of Moss Creek Plantation. As Rebecca sat in line, she saw a car in the next lane with JUST MARRIED painted on the back window. Her thoughts turned to Hunter and the wedding. She couldn't get excited about looking for a wedding gown, and the more time she spent with Hunter, the more she wondered if she'd made the right decision in accepting his proposal and moving from Atlanta. She missed the hustle and bustle of the city, and even more, her old job. And the thought of a huge wedding with hundreds of guests she didn't even know seemed about as appealing as a poke in the eye with a stick.

As hard as she tried, she still had difficulty with the image of melding their lives together. When she'd complained about being disappointed in her new job, Hunter had jumped on the wagon again about her giving up her career and "busying herself with charity work." It wasn't that she was opposed to charity work—as long as someone else was doing it.

Traffic finally began to move at a more reasonable pace once she was through the stoplight.

A few minutes later as she pulled into the parking lot of the Sheriff's Office, she wondered if Morgan and Hassler had gotten anywhere on the hit-and-run case or the Art Grimes murder. She decided if they were in the office, she'd ask what progress they'd made.

Rebecca picked up the daily report for the weekend and ran her finger down the page until she located where Hunter had reported his vehicle stolen. Then she leaned across the counter and smiled at the middle-aged volunteer working the front desk. "Sam, could you let me in the back? I need to ask Shark a question about one of his cases."

"Sure," Sam said as he picked up his cane, slowly made his way to the door, and punched in four numbers on the key pad.

"What happened to you?" Rebecca asked.

"Tore the cartilage in my knee a few days ago playing tennis."

"Sorry to hear that. Thanks for letting me in. You're a doll," Rebecca said as she breezed by him.

As she approached the detective's office, she heard Dell say, "The reason we don't have a report on the trace evidence from the Grimes' murder is that the evidence seems to have been misfiled or something. Anyway, they can't find it."

Rebecca flinched as Shark let go with a string of obscenities that would make a career soldier blush.

She decided perhaps now was not a good time to approach the detectives about anything, so she crept silently back down the hall.

Andrea lay staring at the ceiling tiles in the familiar room at the outpatient clinic. The nurse had finally gotten her IV going after three attempts to find a vein. She pulled off her scarf and laid it on the bed. She reached up and scratched the top of her bald head.

Andrea had convinced Stephanie to stay home and sleep since she had to work that evening. She'd told her she preferred to be alone today. She needed time to think, and with Stephanie hovering over her all the time, she had little opportunity to do so.

What a mess she'd made of her life. She hadn't accomplished any of the goals she'd set for herself. As a child, she'd envisioned her future to be one filled with a husband who couldn't function without her, children who adored her, and a fast-track career. She was batting zero for three. And time was running out.

She wanted to believe the poison dripping slowly into her

veins was going to help, but she knew it wouldn't. If they could find the primary site of her cancer, perhaps it would make a difference. But as her dad used to say with his head stuck under the hood of his old Ford, "You've got to identify what the problem is before you can figure out how to fix it. Otherwise you're just shooting in the dark."

Although she wasn't sure if it was from the cancer or the chemotherapy, she could tell her body was rebelling. It was getting harder to get out of bed and put one foot in front of the other. When she'd stepped on the scales this morning, she found she'd lost another five pounds. Before all this had started, she'd have given her right arm to lose weight. Much more and she'd look like an orphan from Bangladesh.

Now something was going on in her brain. She couldn't think straight sometimes, couldn't verbalize what she was thinking. It was as if the channels kept changing in her mind, and she wasn't in control of the remote. Had the cancer spread there as well? She hadn't mentioned it to Dr. Bartholomeu, afraid he'd want to run more tests and schedule more treatments. Or was it simply a low potassium reading or something less foreboding?

At this point, she wasn't sure it even mattered.

She'd been thinking about God a lot lately, remembering all the stories she'd heard in Sunday school as a child. But her parents' fling with religion hadn't lasted long, and they'd stopped going to church when she was ten. She remembered the story about how Jesus had told the other men crucified with Him that they would join Him in heaven if they only believed. Would He forgive all her sins as well?

"This stupid vehicle could be back in Canada by now," Shark said as he threw his pen across the desk. By mid-afternoon, he'd called all the garages in Savannah, Beaufort, and Hilton Head but had no luck in locating any vehicle with the type of damage he was looking for on the hit-and-run case.

"There were two silver SUVs stolen Friday night: A Lexus that belonged to none other than Rebecca Sand's fiance, Hunter Cowan, and a Honda CRV. I think this case and the Grimes one are going to be bears," Dell said as she stood up and stretched. "At least Brent Grimes is supposed to be back in Savannah tomorrow so we'll get a chance to interview him."

Shark was nodding his head in agreement when the phone rang. "Morgan," he said gruffly.

"Well it sounds like I'm having a better day than you are," Marissa said.

Shark leaned back in his chair. "Sorry about that. How'd the hearing go?"

Dell plopped back down in her chair and observed how quickly Shark's body language changed.

"Great!" Marissa said. "The judge threw the counter-claim out. I won!"

Shark smiled. "I'm sure that's a relief. So where are you?"

"Headed back to the airport. I just passed the turnoff to Hilton Head."

"What time's your flight?"

"Five o'clock. By the time I turn in the rental car and go through security, I shouldn't have long to wait before it'll be time to board."

"Well, you have a good trip. Drop me a postcard every now and then and let me know what's happening with you."

"I'll do that. It was great to see you, and thanks again for the boat ride. It was fun."

"Maybe I'll have a bigger boat by the next time you get back."

Marissa chuckled. "If I have my way, there won't be a next time."

"Never say never."

After Shark hung up, he glanced over at Dell. She rolled her eyes. "What?"

"I thought you said you didn't have any feelings for her anymore."

"I don't!"

"Yeah, keep telling yourself that."

Monique LeBlanc was thankful not to have to deal with her wig and padded clothing on the trip back to Paris. Since she was booked on the same flight as Marissa, it would have been too much of a coincidence if "Babs" was on the same flight.

She whipped her rental car into the turn lane for the Savannah Airport, Marissa three cars ahead of her.

She'd followed Marissa to Charleston on the weekend, but hadn't found a good opportunity to complete her assignment. She was relieved on one hand since murder wasn't really what she'd signed on for, and she considered it a nasty business, but regretted she wouldn't be collecting a fat bonus when her plane landed.

She'd phoned a report to Ears before she left the inn and was relieved when he'd called back and told her not to make any more attempts, that their client had said he would take care of it himself. At least she'd be able to relax on the flight home.

She'd enjoyed her time in the Lowcountry and hoped that Ears would use her for future assignments in the States.

Shark was in bed when the phone rang, and from the looks of his sheets, you would have thought he'd been wrestling a suspect. His eyes darted to the clock on the nightstand and he realized it was almost midnight. He groaned, sure it was the dispatcher. But when he picked up the phone, he was surprised to hear Jazz's voice.

"Were you asleep?" she asked softly.

"No, as a matter of fact I was thinking about you."

"I'm sorry to call so late, but I need to talk."

"Have you reached a decision about the job?"

There was a long pause before Jazz answered. "I've decided to take it. They made me an offer I just couldn't refuse. I talked to my boss today, and I'm going to finish up a couple of cases this week and turn the rest over to an associate. They want me in Washington as soon as possible. I called because I want you to reconsider coming with me."

"Stay here, and marry me instead."

"Shark, we discussed that over the weekend. I don't think I can do that right now."

Shark lay back on the bed and covered his eyes with his arm. "And I don't think I can go with you."

"Let me ask you something. Are you happy here?"

There was a moment of silence before Shark answered. "I'm not sure I know what happy is anymore. But at least I have my job and friends here, and soon I'll be godfather for Dell's baby. It may be the only chance I have to be around a kid, and I don't want to lose that opportunity since it looks like I may never have any of my own."

Jazz blew her nose. Shark could tell she was crying. "So it sounds like I'm not going to be able to talk you into coming with me."

"No, I don't think so. At least not now."

"Will I see you before I leave this weekend?"

Shark paused. "I don't think that's a good idea. It'll only make it harder on both of us, and you've made your decision."

"Shark, I don't want it to end like this between us. Can I call you once I get settled?"

"Of course. And it's not like I'll never see you again. I'm sure you'll be around when the baby is born and for holidays."

"Which will give me a chance to try and twist your arm and change your mind."

"We'll just have to see what happens."

As Shark hung up, he wondered if he was making the biggest mistake of his life.

Chapter Nineteen

Tuesday morning Sheriff Grant strode into the office and slapped a copy of *The Island Packet* onto Shark's desk. "Have you seen this?"

"What?" Dell stood and approached the desk.

"Rebecca Sands's article about how we lost evidence in the Grimes murder case," Grant said, struggling to keep his anger under control. "Is it true?"

"I'm sure it's not lost," Dell answered, "but apparently it has been misplaced. I expect it'll show up any day."

"So how the hell did this reporter find out about it?" Grant asked.

"Why don't I ask her?" Shark said. He yanked his sport coat off the back of his chair.

"Want me to go with you?" Dell asked.

Shark shook his head. "No, I'll handle this."

Dell was grateful. Shark had already been testy since Jazz had decided to take the new job. This was only going to make his mood worse. "You might as well take these pictures to her," Dell said. She picked up an envelope off her desk. "You remember that roll of film she gave you at the scene of the hit-and-run? Well, I had it developed. She bamboozled you. This is her and her fiancé in Charleston, not the pictures she took that day."

Shark snatched the envelope out of Dell's hand and headed for the door.

In the car, he pulled out the photos. Several were of Rebecca and Hunter in the old slave market and at the aquarium, but over half the roll was of them at Folly Beach. Rebecca's white bikini barely covered her essential parts, her hair wet as she walked out of the surf. A good looking broad, no doubt about it. Too bad someone couldn't give her a new personality.

Rebecca was barreling down Highway 278 on her way to the island, when she heard a siren and saw blue lights flashing in the grill of the car that had pulled in behind her.

"Crap!" she said as she slowed and pulled over to the side of the road. She shut off the engine and glanced in the rear view mirror. She was surprised to see Shark hurrying to her vehicle. She rolled down her window.

"Was I speeding?" she asked coyly.

"Yes, but that's not why I stopped you."

"So what's the problem?"

"This," Shark said, thrusting the newspaper at her.

From the crease in his forehead and the squint of his eyes, she could tell he was angry. "I guess that means you didn't like my article. Look, I'm just doing my job."

"And this doesn't make it any easier for me to do mine. So where did you get your information?"

Rebecca looked up at him and grinned. "I don't think you want to know that."

Shark leaned down and rested his arms on the car. "Oh, but I do. Did someone in the department give you that information?"

Rebecca looked him straight in the eye. "Yes."

"Who?"

"You know I can't tell you, and you wouldn't believe me if I did."

"No cop would tell you that—unless he let it slip while playing hanky-panky between the sheets."

"How dare you!" Rebecca said, her hand suddenly in mid-air and drawn back as she prepared to slap him.

Shark caught her wrist. "I wouldn't do that if I were you, unless you want to be arrested for assaulting an officer."

"Let go of me!" Rebecca shouted.

"Gladly. You'd better watch your step or you're going to find yourself in a heap of trouble." As Shark turned to leave, he pulled the envelope of photos out of his coat pocket. He turned back and threw them in the car. "If your bikini gets any smaller you'll be in the slammer for indecent exposure."

"You're just pissed I switched the rolls, and you didn't catch on."

"So tell me, why didn't you plaster the photo of the victim across the front page?"

"Regardless of what you think of me, I do have some principles."

"Who would have guessed?"

Chapter Twenty

Marissa hummed as she turned the key in the lock of her spacious flat the morning after her return from Beaufort. She carried two string bags, one filled with a variety of fresh fruit, which she hefted onto the kitchen bar. The other she set on the counter and began to remove the contents: A tin of mint tea, fresh croissants, a couple of lamb chops, and the ingredients for a Caesar salad. She removed her backpack, which held her drawing pad and pencils.

She filled the kettle and put her groceries away, then emptied the dish drainer and puttered around the kitchen until it was time to pour the hot water into the oriental teapot she'd purchased in Hong Kong.

Carrying a small tray and her backpack down the hall, she entered her studio. It amazed her how her senses seemed to heighten as soon as she had a paintbrush in her hand. She'd started a new painting of the Arc de Triomphe. She'd just spent a couple of hours sitting at an outside cafe on the Champs Elysées sketching the four pillars that supported the structure: The Triumph of Napoleon, Resistance, Peace and The Departure of the Volunteers. She was happy with her outlines of the first three, but she'd had trouble capturing the essence of the last.

She put the tray down on a small table next to her easel then poured the steaming tea into a large mug and added sugar and lemon. Grasping the cup with both hands, she stood studying the section of sky she'd worked on before she'd left for Beaufort. She wasn't completely happy with it and decided to make some adjustments before she went any further.

She set her mug down on the table and crossed the room to turn on the CD player. She liked to listen to Vivaldi's "Four Seasons" or Bach's piano concertos while she painted. The soothing music had just filled the room when she noticed the red light blinking on her answering machine. She grabbed the long blue cotton shirt she wore while painting then went to check her messages.

She punched the play button. "Hello, darling."

Marissa froze. She knew the pleasant life she'd worked so hard to construct for herself was about to be shattered by this voice from her past.

"I've made a reservation for you Friday on American Airlines, flight ten-sixty-nine to Belize. I thought it would be fun to do a little diving, lie on the beach, and check out the Mayan ruins. So wrap up your apartment and business there in Paris and I'll pick you up at the airport."

Marissa wasn't surprised to hear Devon's voice. She'd known the call would come some day. But her good mood suddenly evaporated.

No, *How are you*? No, *I miss you.* No inquiry if this was a convenient time, just a summons.

In the past, she'd always been excited at the prospect of being with Devon again. But she had changed. And her feelings for him had altered, as well. She'd once loved him, or thought she had. Maybe being with him would ignite those feelings again, and they could start enjoying the fruits of their labors. If not, perhaps it was time to split their assets and go their separate ways.

She collapsed onto the small floral loveseat, mourning the loss of her new life and independence she had come to treasure so much.

"How you doing, kiddo?" Stephanie asked when Andrea stumbled into the kitchen.

"Let's just say I'm not sure I agree with that old saying that every day above ground is a good one."

"Sit down, and I'll make you a cup of tea. Think you could eat something? Maybe a piece of dry toast?"

Andrea shook her head. "I'll be lucky to keep the tea down. Did you just get home?"

"Yeah. School started today, and traffic was terrible."

Stephanie picked up her paper plate and threw it in the trash. She'd wanted bacon and eggs but had settled for a bagel, so the smell wouldn't make Andrea nauseated. She put a mug of water into the microwave and set the timer for two minutes.

Andrea leaned on the kitchen table. "It seems silly that they start school in the middle of August. We never used to begin until after Labor Day."

"I know what you mean. So did you get along okay by yourself yesterday and last night?"

"Yes."

"Just think, only two more treatments to go."

"Thank goodness."

Stephanie put the mug of tea on the table in front of Andrea and sat down. She picked up her glass of orange juice and took a sip.

"Andrea, are you okay? I was surprised when you didn't want me to go with you yesterday for your treatment. You said you had some things to think about. Care to share?"

"Not really. I hope you understand."

"It seems like you've had something on your mind the last couple of weeks."

Andrea picked up her mug with both hands. "Other than dying you mean?" she asked sadly.

"I can't begin to imagine what you're going through and the thoughts that must race through your mind. But you seem even more preoccupied than usual."

Andrea thought of the stash of pills she was slowly accumulating. She'd stolen some valium out of the sample closet at one of the doctor's offices when she'd picked up more tapes to transcribe. But when the time came, would she have the nerve to do what she needed to?

"Since we're chatting, can I ask you something?" Andrea asked.

"Sure, shoot."

"You haven't mentioned your father's murder. I know you didn't have any kind of relationship with him, but you didn't go to his funeral or seem to be bothered at all by his murder. Don't you wonder who killed him?"

Stephanie stood up and took another mug out of the cabinet, filled it with water, and placed it in the microwave.

"Just because I haven't talked about it doesn't mean I haven't thought about it. I keep waiting to feel something. Guilt if nothing else."

"Why guilt?"

"That I refused to talk to him when he was dying."

"But you didn't know he was sick."

The bell on the microwave dinged, and Stephanie removed the cup and pulled another tea bag out of the canister. "Even if I had, I don't know if it would have made any difference. He was a terrible man. You have no idea what he put Brent, me, and my mother through."

"You're right, I don't. I was fortunate to have a wonderful childhood. The memories of that are what kept me going after Mom and Dad died."

"I do wonder sometimes about who murdered him. I guess I'm afraid Brent may have been involved, although he said he had nothing to do with it. He has an appointment to talk to the detectives today. I'll feel better when I know he isn't a suspect in their eyes."

Andrea toyed with her spoon. "The newspaper mentioned your father was into gambling. Maybe that caught up with him."

"Could be."

"Do you think the police will ever solve the case?"

"I have no idea. Maybe it's better if they don't. All our past would come out in court. It's better left buried."

Brent Grimes arrived at the sheriff's office a little after one. Shark escorted him to an interview room.

"Mr. Grimes, thank you for agreeing to come in today. We just have a few questions about your father's murder," Shark said.

"No problem. I figured you'd want to talk to me after Stephanie called and told me what happened."

Shark observed the twenty-three-year-old closely. There was a definite family resemblance to Stephanie, although his hair was brown instead of red. Dressed in a pair of khakis and a blue, short-sleeve button-down shirt, he appeared somewhat nervous, his fingers playing a silent melody on the table.

"Stephanie said you're a college student," Dell began.

"Yeah, I'm working on a bachelor's degree in international finance."

"And you live in the dorm?" Shark asked.

"During the school year, but I've been doing a lot of housesitting this summer."

"Had your father contacted you in the past several months?" Dell asked.

"He called several times and wanted to get together, but I didn't want any part of it."

"So you never actually saw him?" Shark asked.

Brent squirmed a little in his chair. "He came into Hugo's, down on River Street, where I bartend a couple of nights a week. Wanted to have a conversation, but I told him to get lost."

"When was this?" Dell asked.

"About a week before he was killed."

"When is the last time you saw him?" Shark asked.

Brent hesitated.

"Do I need to read you your rights?" Shark asked softly.

Brent took a deep breath and let it out slowly. "No, I have nothing to hide. He showed up at the bar the night before he was murdered. He was wasted. Kept insisting he had to talk to me. I told him to get lost, but he refused. Finally, I told the bouncer to throw him out. Unfortunately, he was waiting for me when I got off work. He started yelling at me that he hadn't killed my mother. That he was dying and needed to set things right. I tried to walk away, but he grabbed my arm, and the next thing I knew I had thrown a punch, and he was on the ground. I left him there. That was the last time I saw him."

"What time was that?" Dell asked.

"Around two in the morning."

"And where did you go then?" Shark asked.

"To the professor's place where I'm housesitting."

"Alone?" Dell asked.

"Yes. I was leaving for Key West at six that morning. If I'd known I was going to need an alibi, I would have taken someone home with me."

"Do you own a gun?" Shark asked.

"No."

Dell leaned forward on the table. "Do you know if Stephanie had any contact with your father?"

Brent shifted in the chair and looked over Dell's shoulder at the wall. "She said he called several times, but she refused to see him. That's all I know."

"Growing up, did you or Stephanie ever shoot a gun?" Shark asked.

"We went hunting a few times with grandpa. That's about it."

Attempting to throw him off balance, Dell asked, "The night your mother died, you were at home. Do you think your father was responsible for her death?"

"Absolutely! That's why Steph and I never wanted anything more to do with him. He was an evil man. He delighted in terrorizing others. I'm not sorry he's dead."

They continued the questioning for over an hour.

Once Brent was gone, Dell turned to Shark. "So what do you think?"

"I think most of what he told us is true. Except I think he was lying when he said Stephanie had never met with her father. We know that someone beat up Grimes since he had a broken nose, a cut lip, and two rib fractures. I think old Brent threw more than one punch. Even though he said he doesn't own a gun, maybe he found one at the professor's house. We need to see if the teach has a gun permit and get a warrant to search his house. Also, we need to talk to Stephanie again. I don't like the fact that Brent has no alibi for the time of death or that he conveniently left town the next morning. We've got a lot of work to do."

Chapter Twenty-one

San Francisco

As they entered the hall where the AIDs benefit was being held, Devon Phillips stared openly at the luscious young woman on his arm while multiple photographers snapped their picture. Sabrina Duval was the flavor of the month. At twenty-four, and already a veteran of six films, her face seemed to be on every magazine cover on the stands in San Francisco. Devon had met her when she and her entourage had dined at one of his restaurants.

Captivated from the moment he'd seen her, it had taken all of his charm to get her to have dinner with him a few times and to agree to accompany him to this benefit. He wanted more, so much more.

They were hardly through the front door of the banquet hall when Sabrina turned to him. "David, get me some champagne."

"Devon, not David."

Sabrina giggled. "Of course, so sorry."

Devon reminded himself this was a game she played. It was her way of telling people they weren't important enough for her to remember their names. Sabrina was the first woman he'd ever met who might be better at manipulating people than he was. She was a challenge.

While Devon was waiting in line at the bar, he kept his

eyes fixed on Sabrina. She flirted with everyone—male and female. A brunette, with curly hair down to the middle of her back, her smoky eyes made up like a cat's, her designer gown slit in all the right places, she oozed sexuality.

A few minutes later, champagne glass in hand, he fought his way through the throng of people that surrounded her. "Here you are, darling."

Sabrina wrinkled her forehead and looked down at the flute he held out to her. "Did I ask for champagne? I've changed the my mind. I'd rather have a martini. Be a dear, and get it for me." She turned back to Boy Toy, the rapper she'd been chatting with.

Devon gritted his teeth and returned to the bar. She treated him like a servant, which he understood. He handled Marissa the same way. It was a way of showing control. But he didn't enjoy being on the receiving end. He'd play her game for the moment. With time, he felt confident he could gain an equal footing with dear Sabrina. She was worth the effort.

Devon glanced down at his watch. In a few hours, he'd be in Belize. If all went as planned, he'd be able to take care of his business with Marissa in only a couple of days. He hated to be away from Sabrina. He knew that with her, out of sight was out of mind.

Friday morning Dell shuffled the reports on her desk. "Since the professor said he's never owned a gun, and we didn't find one when we searched his house last night, where do you want to go from here on the Grimes case?"

"Let's talk to Stephanie again. Just because we didn't discover the murder weapon where Brent's staying doesn't mean he isn't involved. He could have bought a gun on the street. If he did, it's probably somewhere between here and Key West. I doubt we'll ever find it."

"I checked and his only arrest was when he was a juvie for joy riding with some of his buddies in one of their parents' cars."

Shark picked up his coffee cup. It was empty. "But with him feeling his father was responsible for his mother's death, and Stephanie telling him old dad had been hassling her, it doesn't take much to imagine him snapping and putting a gun to his father's head. Maybe he felt the need to protect his sister, since he hadn't been able to save his mother. All we need is a fingerprint or something in the trace evidence to place him at the scene, because there's no question he has a motive."

"If they could just locate it. I called again this morning, and they said they're still looking."

Shark yanked open his desk drawer and pulled out his bottle of Tums. "I don't care if they have to tear that building apart and look in every file, we've got to have that evidence. Think I should call them?"

Dell rolled her eyes. "No! They're working on it." She changed the subject trying to ward off the angry outburst she knew was coming. "Let's talk about the Sanchez case for a minute. I've been thinking. Hunter Cowan reported his silver Lexus SUV stolen Friday night. And Rebecca Sands lives in Westbury Park close to where the hit-and-run happened. What if he was on the way to her house, hit Sanchez, realized what he'd done, ditched the car some place, then reported it stolen?"

"That's a pretty big leap, don't you think? I figure his Lexus is on the way to South America or Russia by now. That stolen car ring out of Savannah probably nabbed it," Shark said as he played with his empty coffee cup. "But let's see, Sanchez got off work at eleven, and the autopsy report said the time of death was between one and three in the morning. I doubt he'd be on the way to Sands's house that late. When did Cowan report his vehicle stolen?"

"Saturday morning about eight."

Shark drummed his pencil on the desk. "Where was it stolen from?"

Dell reached for the report. "From his house in Sea Pines."

"I guess we won't know if it was the vehicle involved until it's recovered—if it ever is."

"Geez, can't we have an easy case for a change?" Dell

asked. "On a more personal note, are you going to see Jazz before she leaves this weekend?"

Shark shook his head. "No. It would only make it harder to let her go."

"But maybe you could persuade her to stay."

"And have her resent me for standing in her way? No thanks."

"Well, maybe she'll get up there and decide she doesn't like it," Dell said as she picked up her empty teacup. "I'm gonna get a refill. Want one?"

"Nah, I've had enough caffeine. Just bring me some water."

Dell stood up and stretched. "So who do you think gave Sands the info about the Grimes evidence?"

Shark's brow furrowed. "Beats me. She said it was some-one in the department though. Have you seen her hanging out with anyone or heard any of the officers talking about her?"

"No, not at all. You mean you couldn't charm the infor-mation out of her?"

"Fat chance. She's the most despicable woman I've come across in a long time."

"You'd better watch it. They say there's a fine line between love and hate."

Shark threw a Post-It pad at her. She ducked and slipped into the hall.

Andrea was transcribing her tapes when the doorbell rang. She hurried to the door so it wouldn't wake Stephanie.

"Is Miss Grimes home?" Shark asked.

"Yes, but she's asleep."

"Please get her up," Shark said as he and Dell stepped into the foyer.

Andrea slipped into Stephanie's room and shook her awake. "The cops are here and want to talk to you."

"Keep them busy while I get dressed and run a comb through my hair."

Andrea returned to the living room. "She'll be right out. Would you like something to drink?"

"No thanks," Dell said as Shark waved his hand.

"Has something happened?" Andrea asked as she sat down in the rocker.

Dell noted Andrea's pale face and the dark circles under her eyes. It was hard not to stare at her bald head.

Stephanie entered the room and sat down in an armchair. "Detectives, what's up?"

Shark turned to Andrea. "We'd like to speak to Stephanie in private. Would you mind?"

"Oh. I'll just go in the bedroom."

Shark waited until he heard the door close. "Stephanie, you know we spoke with your brother yesterday. We found some discrepancies in your statement."

Stephanie had talked to Brent after his interview and couldn't figure out what they were referring to.

Shark leaned forward. "We know you lied to us when you said you hadn't seen your father."

"Did Brent tell you I had?"

"It doesn't matter what Brent told us. I'll ask you again, did you have any contact with your father? And bear in mind that if you lie to us, and we have a witness that can prove you did see him, then it will only make us more suspicious."

Stephanie chewed on her lip, trying to figure out if they were bluffing or if someone had seen them together.

Andrea was listening at the bedroom door. Her palms were clammy as she waited to hear how Stephanie would answer the question.

Stephanie took a deep breath. "He showed up at work one morning and tried to force me into his car. I fought him off and hid in the underground parking garage until he left."

"Why did you lie to us earlier?" Dell asked.

"I was afraid it would look like I had a motive to kill him—and I didn't do it."

"What did your brother say when you told him about it?" Shark asked.

Stephanie hung her head. "He said not to worry. That everything would be okay."

Dell touched Stephanie's knee and asked softly, "What did you think he meant by that?"

Stephanie looked at Dell. "That he would talk to him and get him off my back. That's all."

"Do you think Brent killed your father?" Shark asked.

"No!"

"Did you know Brent had a fight with him the night he was murdered? That he broke your father's nose and fractured a couple of his ribs?"

"I didn't know about the fight until yesterday. He said he only threw one punch," Stephanie said as tears began to stream down her cheeks. "I shouldn't have told him."

Dell grabbed a tissue out of the box on the coffee table and handed it to Stephanie. "Does your brother own a gun?"

"Not that I know of."

Shark stood up. "I think that's all for now. We'll let ourselves out."

As soon as Andrea heard the door close, she burst out of the bedroom and raced to Stephanie. "Are you okay?"

"No, I think they're going to arrest Brent for murdering my father."

Marissa stored her carry-on in the overhead bin and relaxed into the plush leather seat in first class. When the flight attendant approached, she accepted a glass of champagne, kicked off her shoes, and slipped on the footies the airline provided. She smoothed the wrinkles from her silk skirt, wanting to look her best when she arrived in Belize.

As she'd thought about Devon's summons, she'd become increasingly suspicious of his motive, especially in light of the fact she was the only one who knew of his crimes and could put him in jail.

The more she thought about it, the more paranoid she had become. So much so that she'd paid a visit to her solicitor and written a new will, and dashed off a letter to Shark with instructions on the envelope that if she didn't contact him by a certain date, then he was to open the letter. At least if something did happen to her, they would know that Devon was responsible.

She had mixed feelings about seeing Devon. She'd enjoyed her independence in France, the first opportunity to be entirely on her own and accountable to no one. But she was anxious to see if the old spark was still there with Devon, and to finally share the wealth they'd accumulated. All their years of planning were about to come to fruition.

The last time they'd been together was in El Hierro just off the coast of Spain. It was there he'd informed her of their next mark, a wealthy oil baroness in San Francisco. And he'd promised this one would be their last. Once they added her fortune to what they'd already accumulated, they would never have to work again. They could finally be together for the rest of their lives. She'd longed for their unsavory business to be over so they could be free from it all, but now that the time had come, she wasn't sure she was still in love with Devon and interested in a future together.

Marissa sipped her champagne and thought back to how it had all started. Devon had taken a naive girl from Hazard, Kentucky, and introduced her to the finer things in life. He'd squired her to museums and art galleries, symphonies and the ballet. He had worked with her to lose her coarse accent. It was as if she'd been Eliza Doolittle and had been magically transformed by Devon into a woman with class. In the process, Devon also made her totally dependent upon him. He'd dictated the smallest details of her life, from the way she wore her hair to the style of her clothes.

For Marissa's part, she would have done anything to please him. She needed Devon to validate her, not only as a woman, but also as a person. She hadn't felt whole unless she was with him. He was the first man who ever paid any attention to her, the only one to love her. And since her parents' death just before she went off to college, he was her sole lifeline.

Shortly after they were married their junior year in college, Devon began to talk about what he wanted out of life, things a girl from Kentucky had never even fantasized about. Houses in the Caribbean and Europe, traveling the world

and collecting priceless art. He dreamed of owning a vineyard in France, cases of slender wine bottles bearing his
name. He wanted to enjoy life, not get worn out by it.

Gradually Marissa came to believe it might be possible,
this waking fantasy. The night he told her how they could
achieve all those things, she hadn't believed he was serious.
They'd been drinking all evening, and she was sure it was
the wine talking. But slowly, over time, Devon had worn
down her reluctance. He'd finally convinced her that, after
all, she wouldn't be the one taking the risks. All she would
have to do was be her beautiful, charming self. Devon would
be the producer and director, Marissa, simply an actor playing a part. Then, after a couple of performances, they would
have enough money to spend the rest of their lives fulfilling
their dreams. When he put it that way, how could she refuse?

Their first mark had been a large landowner in Kentucky,
and after his untimely death, Marissa inherited his entire
estate. Shortly thereafter, Devon had married a wealthy
widow, who was lost at sea on their honeymoon.

Then there was Marcus DeSilva, a millionaire real estate
developer on Hilton Head Island. Marissa was fearful they
were going to get caught that time, not realizing until they
hooked up on El Hierro that things were not as they
appeared. Shark's partner, Dell, had become suspicious. But
as hard as Dell tried, she hadn't been able to establish a con-
tinuing connection between Marissa and Devon. Now with
the death of Devon's latest wife, anyone who looked closely
would definitely see a pattern. However, she admired
Devon's careful planning. The "incidents" occurred in different parts of the country, and there had been no apparent
communication between the two of them since their divorce
shortly after they graduated from college. Finally, it was all
over now. It was time to get on with their lives together and
realize some of those dreams they'd worked so hard for.
Devon had been right—his plan had worked flawlessly.

But in the past year, Marissa knew she'd changed. For the
first time in her life there'd been no man ruling her every
action, and as frightening as it was at first, she'd come to
enjoy it. She'd loved setting up house and decorating her flat

in Paris; cutting her hair short, which Devon would never have allowed; wearing jeans and an old cotton shirt as she painted instead of the designer clothes Devon had insisted on. She felt she'd finally found her true self and not the mask she always assumed when she was playing a role. Deep down inside, she knew that the unsophisticated girl from Hazard, Kentucky, still lurked.

Although she'd missed Devon, she realized as she reflected on the past that he'd always treated her as he would a pet that performed well. She wasn't sure if she was ready for that again. Would he be willing to consider her an equal now? What did their future hold? Did he still love her?

Chapter Twenty-two

Shark and Dell were crossing the parking lot in Coligny Plaza shopping center on their way back from lunch when they bumped into Stephanie and Andrea coming out of Chico's clothing store.

"Miss Grimes, Miss Michaels," Shark said. "Looks like you've been doing a little shopping."

"Andrea's lost so much weight from her treatments she needs a new wardrobe."

"I hope things are going well," Dell said as she admired the blond wig that Andrea was wearing. "That hairstyle looks good on you."

"Thanks," Andrea said reaching up and touching the shoulder-length hair. "It's a little longer than my real hair was before the treatments."

Andrea had barely finished her sentence before Stephanie blurted out, "I guess you didn't come up with anything more on Brent since he's still free."

"Not yet, but we're still working on it," Shark said.

"I told you he didn't do it."

"I saw in the newspaper that you lost some of the evidence," Andrea said.

"You can't believe everything you read in the papers," Dell said defensively.

"It doesn't really matter to me whether you solve it or not," Stephanie said as she turned away.

"It matters to me," Shark said softly.

After the girls were out of earshot, Dell turned to Shark. "I feel so sorry for Andrea. Doesn't she look awful? The treatments must not be working."

Marissa was surprised by the pleasant temperature and lack of humidity when she stepped off the plane in Belize. Her attention was drawn to a large transport plane parked a short distance away and armed soldiers running around in camouflage.

"What's going on over there?" Marissa asked the flight attendant who was standing at the bottom of the stairs.

"Nothing to worry about. This used to be an English colony. And they still use it as a tropical training ground for their troops."

Relieved that a coup wasn't about to take place, Marissa entered the small brick terminal.

Devon sauntered across the room, enveloped her in his arms, and squeezed her tightly. "Hi, sweetheart. Let me look at you. You cut your hair, but you're still gorgeous. Did you have a good flight?"

Marissa had been curious to see how she would feel when she saw Devon again after all this time. That old rush of passion and excitement that she'd always felt in past meetings was missing.

Marissa smiled up at him. "It was fine. Have you been here long?"

"No, my flight got in about twenty minutes ago. Come on, let's get this paperwork over with so we can get out of here." They entered a large room where they were instructed to fill out forms to declare what they were bringing into the country, where they were from, and how long they would be staying.

Once they finished, Devon handed their passports and return airline tickets to the official at the counter.

"Most businesses will accept U.S. dollars," the clerk said as he stamped the seal of his country onto their passports. "If not, you can exchange them at any bank."

Marissa was relieved to see that English was the major language, along with a mixture of Creole and Spanish.

"We've booked a flight on to Ambergris Caye," Devon said. "Can you tell me where we catch that plane?"

"Go down the hall, turn left. It will be the third counter on your right. Enjoy your stay in our country."

"Have you been here before?" Marissa asked as they hurried to catch their connecting flight.

"A couple of days a few years ago."

Marissa wondered which of his former wives he'd taken on that trip.

A short time later, they boarded a small eight-seater and flew north out of Belize City. Marissa was astonished to see that mangrove trees surrounded the entire coast outside of the settlements.

Once they landed at Ambergris, which was the largest of the cayes, they took a taxi to San Pedro, which Devon said attracted more visitors than the rest of the country combined.

The sun was low on the horizon by the time they checked into one of the new condominiums that had recently sprung up on the beach. Expecting something lavish, Marissa was disappointed to find it was typical of most middle-class beachside places she'd stayed in. She'd discovered in her travels that they all seemed to look alike.

Marissa opened the sliding glass door onto the deck so she could hear the surf and take advantage of the cool breeze. About a hundred yards from shore, the waves broke over the reef. The sky was streaked with purple and orange as the last slice of sun disappeared. Tall palm trees lined the curving white beach.

Devon walked up behind her, slipped his arms around her waist, and nuzzled her ear. "I've missed you." He turned her around and lowered his lips to hers.

She willed herself not to respond, but her body had a mind of its own. It was as if her suspicions had suddenly evaporated like dew on a morning rose.

Devon rubbed his hands gently across her back. Marissa looked up at him. Blue eyes the color of a robin's egg held hers transfixed. He kissed her again, deeply, possessively, causing her to lean in closer to him. Suddenly he broke off the kiss and nibbled on her earlobe.

"Let's go find something to eat. I'm starved. Then we can come back and relax. Tomorrow we can shop for some fresh fruit and supplies."

"Do I have time to take a shower?"

"Let's wait until we get back. Even though it's the beginning of tourist season, I don't know how late the restaurants will stay open. Do you want to walk down the beach or drive the golf cart?"

"Golf cart?"

"Yes, it comes with the condo. As you probably noticed, the streets are all dirt here on the caye, and the rainy season just ended, so they're filled with mud. Everyone drives golf carts."

Marissa didn't like the idea of walking down the beach after dark. "I'd like to see the town, if that's okay with you."

Devon chuckled. "I wouldn't exactly call it a town. There's one main street where all the restaurants and tourist shops are located."

As they drove slowly down the muddy street, Marissa gazed at small thatched huts that sold everything from T-shirts, postcards, and bathing suits to replicas of various Mayan ruins. They passed a small Catholic church practically overrun with blooming bougainvillea. A couple of tiny restaurants looked as if they catered to locals. Devon finally pulled up in front of The Howler.

"That's an interesting name," Marissa commented as she stepped out of the golf cart.

"This is one of the few places in the world that still has howler monkeys. They're an endangered species. Only a few left in Belize, southern Mexico, and isolated areas of Guatemala. They have this loud, rasping howl, which can be heard for over a mile. You'll see some up at the Mayan ruins."

Marissa swatted at a horde of mosquitoes that assaulted her as they hurried toward the entrance. Once inside, she was shocked to see that the floor was also dirt, but at least it was dry. A small boy, probably no more than ten years old, led them to a table at the rear and handed them menus.

"You have to be careful what you drink here, just like in

Mexico. Stick to bottled water, soda, or wine," Devon said as he perused the selections. "Why don't I order for both of us?"

"Great." Marissa closed her menu, which was handwritten on a piece of white construction paper.

When their waiter appeared, Devon ordered a Chilean red wine and a host of dishes. "And make sure nothing is cooked in peanut oil. I'm allergic to peanuts," Devon said.

"*Si*, I tell cook."

Marissa observed three other couples, probably Americans, at a table across the room. To her right, two young men who spoke French discussed their dive of the day. She smiled at the familiar sound of the language. A handsome, middle-aged man of obvious Spanish descent occupied the only other table. He returned her gaze then smiled and lifted his glass to her. Embarrassed, she turned back to Devon.

Devon noted the interplay between Marissa and the Spaniard and chuckled. "I see you haven't lost your ability to attract attention even with that short hair."

Before Marissa could say anything, their waiter returned with their wine and an appetizer. Once he'd filled their glasses and placed the food in front of them, he hurried to greet some new arrivals. Looking at the concoction on her plate, Marissa asked, "What's this?"

"A fish taco."

Marissa looked up at him. "That doesn't sound too appealing."

"It's amazingly good. Try it. You'll like it."

Marissa took a sip of wine before she reached for the taco. Devon watched as she bit into it and wasn't surprised when she began to smile.

"You're right. This is wonderful."

When she finished, Devon took her hand. "I'm so glad you're here. It's going to be fun to relax a little and get reacquainted. And I think we can finally start making some plans for the future."

"Do you think it's been long enough since your wife died that we won't arouse suspicion?"

"Absolutely. Especially since she died of 'natural causes.' I've squired an occasional female to various charity events since then, and it hasn't seemed to raise any eyebrows."

As they feasted on baked mahi-mahi, rice, and beans, Marissa listened as Devon talked about his restaurants and his catering business. "I kind of like having the three most popular dining places in town. Ashley Balmore was in last night with her whole entourage. And Clay Grant and all his bodyguards were at the Eagle's Nest the other night."

"Who's Clay Grant?" Marissa asked.

"He's a huge movie star. Don't tell me you haven't heard of him. I'll have to take you around and show you my little empire. I think you'll be impressed."

Marissa doubted it. Maybe in the past, when she was that shy girl from Kentucky, but not anymore. She'd dined in some of the finest restaurants in the world. "I can understand why you find it exciting that everyone knows you and frequents your establishments, but Devon, now that all the sordid business is behind us and we've attained our goal of financial security, I'm ready to discuss the future."

"Obviously you've been thinking about things. So tell me, where do you see us going from here?"

Marissa played with the base of her wine glass. "You used to talk about your dream of owning a vineyard in France."

"I've been rethinking that. They have perfectly good ones in Napa."

Marissa's head snapped up. "Are you saying you want to stay in San Francisco?"

"Maybe."

"When you can choose anywhere in the world to live?"

"What about you? Have you picked out some place special?"

"I thought we would be making that decision together. I loved Spain, and I would like to spend some time in Greece. I *don't* want to remain in the States. And I think it would be safer if we lived abroad."

"If you're so concerned about the stupid cops figuring everything out, why did you go see that detective when you were in South Carolina?" Devon immediately regretted the question.

Marissa sat back in her chair as if she'd been hit in the chest. *How does he know I saw Shark?*

"I stopped by his house to drop off a picture I had painted, when he pulled into the driveway. I hadn't really planned on seeing him."

"That doesn't explain why you spent the evening with him out on his boat."

"How do you know that?"

Devon smiled. "Oh, a little birdie told me."

"Have you had someone following me the whole time we've been apart?"

Devon shook his head. "Of course not. I just thought it might be a good idea while you were back in South Carolina since you seem to have a soft spot for that cop."

Marissa didn't believe him. He had to be keeping tabs on her to even know she went to Beaufort. She decided not to press the issue. She figured it was part of Devon's need to control her. She hoped to change that soon. To show him she had grown into an independent woman every bit his equal.

Marissa pushed her plate aside. "He was kind to me when Marcus was murdered and after my car accident. He's one of the primary reasons I think we should live abroad. I can just see us staying in San Francisco, then stumbling across Shark or his partner vacationing somewhere out there. They were suspicious enough after Marcus died. Can you imagine what they would think if they found us together?"

"That's pretty unlikely, don't you think? And what would it matter if they did? We didn't do old Marcus in."

"Anyway, I prefer to live abroad."

Devon threw up his hands. "Well then, okay. Why are we even discussing it? I think it's time for dessert."

"What did you order?" Marissa asked.

"Fried plantain."

"What's that?"

"It looks like a big green banana. You've probably seen them in grocery stores. Anyway, they roll it in a sugary batter then deep fry it." Devon picked up his wine glass and swirled the dark liquid around. "Trust me. You'll like it. I thought we'd stay here at San Pedro for two days then move inland. Tomorrow we can rent some diving gear and head out to the reef. There's some of the best diving in the world here."

A knot formed in Marissa's stomach. "I'm not a very good diver. I've gone only a few times, and I haven't been down at all since we were on El Hierro. How about we start with some snorkeling?"

"You'll be fine. It's like riding a bike."

Marissa played with the cork from the wine. They'd almost finished the bottle, and she was beginning to feel the effects. "Maybe we should go in a group or take a dive instructor with us."

Devon frowned. "I'd rather explore on our own. What are you afraid of anyway?"

Marissa picked up the wine bottle and divided the remainder between their two glasses, stalling. "Nothing, just trying to be cautious, especially since we're not familiar with the local waters."

"Well, I've been diving for years. The water here is crystal clear. It's not like I won't be able to see you if you have a problem."

Marissa didn't say anything further. She knew it wouldn't matter anyway.

Their dessert came, and it was better than Marissa had anticipated. Devon devoured his with just a few bites. "After we get our fill of diving, while we're still on the coast, I want to go up to a resort north of here so we can do some bone fishing for a couple of days."

"I've never heard of a bone fish."

"It's one of the most difficult fish in the world to catch. They're small. Only weigh a few pounds, but they swim twenty-seven miles per hour. They can rip off one hundred yards of line in one to two seconds—like an underwater rocket."

"How far out do you have to go to catch them?"

Devon chuckled. "It's fly fishing. You go to flats and wade in a few feet of water."

"I'm not much of a fisherman."

"Just try it. Maybe you'll like it."

At that point, Marissa knew Devon wasn't going to let her out of his sight.

Devon ordered a couple of bottles of wine to be added to their bill then settled up with their waiter.

On the short drive to the condo, Marissa could hear loud music blaring from a couple of the local hangouts. "Doesn't this remind you of Key West with all the bars and tourist stuff?"

"A poor Key West maybe."

When they entered the condo, Marissa sat down on the white wicker sofa. "So besides diving and snorkeling, what else is there to do around here?"

Devon picked up a brochure of activities off the coffee table. "Sailing and wind surfing. One of the places I want to take you diving is the Blue Hole. If we have time, I'd like to go tubing through the caves along the Chiquibul River. The last time I was here, there was some kind of mineral leeching from the rocks. The guide said it was very irritating to the skin, so I skipped it. Oh, and I want to show you the ruins, of course."

Devon drew a small package out of his pocket and extended it to her. "For you."

Marissa tore the gold paper off and discovered a beautiful ruby and diamond necklace. In spite of the Tiffany box it came in, she wondered if it had been the oil baroness's. "Thank you. It's beautiful."

"Come here and let me put it on you," Devon said.

Marissa sat beside him on the couch while he fastened the necklace. He kissed the nape of her neck. "I need to make a couple of calls and check on how everything's going at the restaurants. Why don't you go ahead and get in the shower, and I'll join you shortly."

As Marissa let the warm water play onto the stiff muscles in her neck, she replayed the evening in her mind. It had felt good to be kissed and held again. She had missed that living alone. She found herself excited at the prospect of starting a new life together. Devon had treated her fairly well today. But she didn't like the fact that he'd had her followed in Beaufort. Had he let that slip inadvertently, or did he want her to know that he was aware of her every move? She also didn't like the sound of caves, ruins, and blue holes especially since Devon's second wife had had an "accident" while they were sailing on their honeymoon. Or was she being paranoid? He didn't need her anymore as a partner for his schemes, and she was the only one on the face of the earth who knew he'd murdered three people.

Chapter Twenty-three

Shark and Dell stood over the headless, bloated torso that had washed up onto South Beach at the tip of the island in Sea Pines Plantation. In addition to the head, the left leg and right arm were missing. A brown leather belt was cinched around the waist but only remnants of a pair of pants remained.

"Is it Gus Manley?" Dell asked.

"I imagine so. At least now his wife can give what's left of him a decent burial." Dell wrinkled her nose. "Do you think the head will show up?"

Shark wiped the sweat dripping into his eyes on the arm of his shirt. "I doubt it. I'm surprised this much washed ashore."

Dell shook her head. "It must be awful to find out your loved one has been eaten by sharks. That would give me nightmares."

"I know, but I think it would be better than never knowing for sure what happened. Why don't you go find some shade? I don't want you passing out from the heat."

"I'm all right."

"Hey guys!" Anna Connors called as she joined them. "Looks like there's not much left of this one."

"Can you hurry your exam along so we can get this body off the beach?" Shark asked, turning to look over his shoulder at the throng of people behind the crime scene tape.

"Shouldn't take long," Anna said as she stooped down. She quickly perused the scene and took a couple of photos. "Help me turn the body over. According to Gus's wife, he has a small scar on his left buttock."

Dell took a step back, so Shark leaned over and helped Anna.

A few seconds passed before Anna confirmed it was Gus. "Did you know him?" she asked.

Shark shook his head. "Not really. Our paths crossed a few times at fishing tournaments."

Anna motioned for the paramedics to approach. "Well, the tourists will sure have a story to tell when they get home."

Shark's cell phone rang. He reached for it, listened for a moment, then hung up. He turned to Dell. "We need to get back to the office. They found Hunter Cowan's car at the Savannah airport, and it looks like it may be the vehicle involved in the hit-and-run."

Sunday afternoon Rebecca, wrapped in Hunter's bathrobe, stood in his kitchen, the glow of lovemaking still lighting up her face. She was humming as she prepared a tray of cheese and crackers. The sudden and sustained ringing of the doorbell startled her.

"I'll get it," Hunter called from the bedroom. He grabbed his pants off the floor and pulled them on. He didn't bother with a shirt. The bell rang again insistently.

Hunter hurried to the front door and yanked it open. He didn't recognize the man and woman on his doorstep. He was about to ask if the house was on fire or make some other glib remark, when he noticed the couple was not smiling. "Can I help you?"

"Are you Hunter Cowan?" the man asked.

"Yes."

"I'm Detective Morgan, and this is my partner, Dell Hassler. We need to speak with you. Can we come in?"

"Is there a problem?" Hunter asked.

"I don't think you want to discuss it on your doorstep. Unless you don't mind the whole neighborhood hearing your business," Shark said sharply.

Hunter opened the door wider. "Please come in."

Rebecca entered the foyer and almost dropped the plate in her hand when she saw Shark and Dell. "What are you guys doing here?"

"Mr. Cowan's car has been recovered at the Savannah airport, and we need to have a word with him," Dell said.

Shark had difficulty looking away from Rebecca. Her hair tousled, obviously fresh from a romp in the hay, elicited unexpected feelings.

"Becca will show you to the living room. I'll just get a shirt and be right with you," Hunter said as he dashed down the hall.

Even though she was embarrassed in Hunter's robe, Rebecca didn't feel she could excuse herself to get dressed until Hunter returned.

"Right this way," she said as she led them to the formal living room. She motioned for them to have a seat on the couch and sank into a high-backed chair. She readjusted the top of the robe a little and placed the plate of cheese and crackers on the coffee table. "Would you like one?" she asked, motioning to the plate.

"No thanks," Shark said, and Dell waved her hand.

Attempting to fill the silence, Rebecca said, "It's great news that you recovered Hunter's car. Although he's already bought a new toy—a Porsche."

Hunter returned and sat down in a chair next to the couch. He picked up a cracker, sat back, and crossed his legs. "I can't believe you found my car. I figured it was long gone."

Shark observed that Hunter seemed to have difficulty making eye contact with him. And although Hunter tried to project an air of indifference, his fingers drummed nervously on the arm of the chair. "Yeah, we were surprised too, especially since it seems to be the vehicle involved in the hit-and-run of Tomas Sanchez."

Rebecca's hand clutched the top of her robe. "Oh no!"

Hunter looked from the detectives to Rebecca. "Who is Tomas Sanchez?"

"The Hispanic man who was hit out by Rose Hill Plantation a little over a week ago," Dell replied.

"You remember me telling you about it?" Rebecca asked her fiancé.

"Oh yes. Now I know who you're talking about."

"Can you tell us where you were that night?" Shark asked.

Hunter's head snapped up. "You can't think I was involved."

"You didn't answer the question," Dell said.

Hunter leaned forward in his chair. "I was at home."

"He called and left a message on my answering machine," Rebecca piped up.

Shark turned to her. "Did you speak to him anytime that evening?"

Rebecca shook her head. "I don't think so. That was the day of the field trip for the Citizens' Police Academy. I had to cover several events and didn't get home until late that evening. It's hard to remember if I called him that night or the next morning."

"How do you know it was my car that was involved?" Hunter asked.

"From the damage to the right front fender and head light—and some tissue was sucked into the engine," Shark said.

No one spoke for a moment.

"Can anyone vouch for your whereabouts that night?" Dell asked.

Hunter shook his head. "No, I was home alone."

"Did you speak to anyone on the phone late that evening?" Shark asked.

Hunter picked a piece of lint off his shirtsleeve. "What time are you talking about? I can hardly remember who I talked to yesterday, let alone a week ago."

"The accident occurred around two or three in the morning," Rebecca said defiantly. "Who would you expect him to be talking to that time of the morning?"

Shark turned to Rebecca. "You?"

Hunter chuckled. "Hardly. Once she falls asleep, the building could collapse around her, and she'd never know."

Shark stood up abruptly. "I guess that's all for now. We can check your phone records. We'll let ourselves out."

As soon as they were back in the car, Dell asked, "What gives? You hardly questioned him."

"No need to. I could tell from his body language that he knows more than he's letting on. Either he was driving—or he knows who was."

"I got the same impression. I'll start checking with cab companies and courtesy vans from the airport."

"Also, run his cell phone records. He could've called a friend to come and pick him up."

"Are you sure you just don't want him to be the guilty party? I saw the way you looked at Sands."

Shark rolled his eyes. "Give me a break. They deserve each other."

Monday morning Andrea sat in her doctor's office hopeful that she would hear good news regarding her latest test results.

Dr. Bartholomeu shuffled the papers in front of him. Finally, he pulled off his gold wire-rimmed glasses and laid them on the desk. He ran his hand through his white hair and cleared his throat.

"I was optimistic the new round of chemotherapy would accomplish what the last had not, decrease the level of HCG hormone in your blood. However, it appears your body is not responding to the treatment. I know with each dose your side effects get worse, which is not unexpected with the cumulative effects of the medications. At this point, I don't think there's any reason to subject you to the last two treatments."

Tears spilled onto Andrea's cheeks. She closed her eyes, took a deep breath, and tried to keep her emotions under control. She wasn't surprised by the news. In her heart, she knew the deadly cocktail of medications wasn't helping, that her time was running out.

Dr. Bartholomeu gave her a moment before he continued. "I don't understand why nothing seems to be working and we can't identify the primary site of your cancer. If we could, perhaps it would enable us to design an effective treatment program. I'm sorry, Andrea. I'd like to send you up to Duke or to MD Anderson's Cancer Institute in Texas. I've already been on the phone with doctors at both places. They're willing to see you immediately. MD Anderson has an experimental program they may be able to get you into."

Andrea shook her head. "Why? So they can repeat all the tests and poke me full of more holes? Spend my last days in a hospital puking my guts out from another wonder drug, not able to see the sun or hear the birds sing? No, I don't think so. I'd rather live a few days less and try and enjoy the time I have left. So how much longer do I have?"

Dr. Bartholomeu stroked his mustache. He could tell he wasn't going to be able to change her mind and thought that, under similar circumstances, he might have made the same decision. "Honestly, I have no idea. I've never run across a case quite like yours. I wish I could be more helpful."

Andrea stood up. "Well, don't take this personally, Doc, but I hope I never see you again. I've had about all the hospitals and doctors I can stand. But thanks for trying."

Dr. Bartholomeu stood and moved to her side. Andrea could see tears crowding his eyes.

"I'm so sorry we failed you. Live a lifetime in the next few months, Andrea. You deserve that and a whole lot more."

"Thanks," she said as she turned away.

Chapter Twenty-four

After a couple of days of waiting for Devon to make a move, Marissa had begun to relax. He'd had ample opportunities to drown her, throw her overboard, and kill her in a dozen different ways. They'd spent two days diving and sailing and now were at the fishing resort. The first day she'd been so afraid she hadn't been able to enjoy the beauty of the reef. But by the time they'd taken a charter over to Blue Hole, one of only three coral atolls in the Western Hemisphere, she'd begun to enjoy herself.

She rolled over on the chaise lounge and untied her bikini top. The bright colors of the Bird of Paradise plants growing in pots around the perimeter of the deck attracted numerous hummingbirds. The sun was bright, and the breeze rustled the fronds of the palm trees. The hypnotic sound of the surf caressed her.

Devon was off fishing for tarpon, and it felt good to have some time to herself and be able to let her guard down.

He'd wanted her to join him, but she'd begged off to lie on the beach and work on her tan. One day of wading in water up to her knees and swatting mosquitoes the size of small planes was enough for her. Fighting a large fish for hours sounded about as much fun as a hysterectomy. However, she'd noticed Devon had taken both of their passports and airline tickets and left her only a twenty-dollar bill. Although they were making progress, he apparently still didn't trust her.

Nevertheless, things seemed to be going well considering the amount of time they'd spent apart. She and Devon had laughed, loved, and had a wonderful time so far. It reminded her of when they'd first been dating in college, except now they didn't have to pool their change to buy a cheap bottle of wine, or play gin rummy because they couldn't afford to take in a movie. Devon's wit and charm were disarming. She hadn't laughed so much in a long time. She'd missed that when she lived alone in France, the laughter and companionship. Days would go by, and her only contact with people would be when she went out to buy fresh fruit and croissants or ventured out to art class or her flying lesson. Looking back, she realized how much she'd isolated herself. She'd escaped into her painting, so she didn't have to think about her unhappy childhood or the lives that she and Devon had destroyed.

Her part had been easy, almost too easy. After her make-over by Devon she'd never had trouble attracting the attention of any man she'd wanted to meet. He'd give her the name of the mark, and it was up to her to get his attention. Once she did, it wasn't long before things would progress quickly.

She thought of Eric, their first victim, whom she'd grown fond of during the eighteen months they were married. She'd been afraid of horses, until Eric taught her to ride. Six months into the marriage, she'd been stunned to find she was pregnant, especially since she had an IUD, something Devon had insisted on. But she had miscarried a short time later. How shocked Devon would have been if a child had foiled his plans. She knew he would have insisted she abort the baby—but that was the one thing she would have defied him on. She would have kept the secret from him until it was too late. She wondered what her life would have been like if she hadn't lost the child and Eric hadn't died.

One of Devon's rules was she would never know when the "accident" would happen, so she'd be genuinely distressed when the police interviewed her, and she had been.

Marissa retied her bikini top, stood up, and wiped the perspiration from her brow. She strolled down the steps and across the coarse white sand, careful to give a couple of iguanas a wide berth, and plunged into the tepid water, allowing it not only to cool her, but also put her memories back into storage.

Late that afternoon, Marissa drove the golf cart down to the tourist shops and searched for some drawing materials. All she found was a small sketchpad and some colored pencils. She asked for a couple of sodas and was surprised to find the Coca Colas were in old-fashioned small bottles and that the bottles looked about a hundred years old. Noticing her expression, the vendor explained that they recycled them. At least they were cold, Marissa thought.

She wandered among the stalls and found a silver bracelet with a small vial she could fill with perfume. She counted how much money she had left and was pleased to see she had enough for the bracelet and the other item she was purchasing.

Back at the condo, Marissa pulled a chair into the shade on the deck and began sketching the beach scene with the fishing boats in the distance. An hour later, she heard the door open.

"Hey, hey! Look what I've got," Devon said as he carried a large, smelly fish out to show her. "How about grouper for dinner?"

"For half the caye?"

Devon laughed. "Isn't he a beauty? I know it's more than we can eat. I'm going to take it down to the market and find someone to clean it and cut us a couple of nice filets."

"What are you going to do with the rest?"

"Let the guy have whatever we don't need. He'll probably be able to feed his whole family for a couple of days. I just wanted to show it to you first."

Marissa closed her sketchpad. "So, did you catch any tarpon?"

"I had one hooked but lost him the second time he jumped out of the water."

"Sounds like you had a good time."

"It was great! I'll be back in a few minutes."

"Find out how we're supposed to cook it and if we need any special spices while you're at the market."

"Will do."

After he left, Marissa put down her sketching pencil and thought about Devon. He seemed so happy since they'd been here. Maybe this would convince him he didn't need the headache of the restaurants, and they could get on with their lives together as she'd originally hoped. The future was the one thing they hadn't discussed since that first night over dinner. She knew he'd made several business calls each day, and she often heard him swearing and yelling at whoever happened to be the unfortunate person on the other end of the line. One would think he'd relish the idea of getting away from all the stress. Maybe tonight after dinner would be the time to bring it up.

Devon returned an hour later, placed the filets in the refrigerator, then took a quick shower.

They baked the fish in coconut milk and made a fresh lime sauce to serve with it. Devon pulled the small kitchen table out onto the deck. Marissa found a candle in a dresser drawer in the bedroom.

There was little conversation as they ate. "This is wonderful," Marissa said as she wiped her hands on her napkin.

"It sure put up a good fight. I fought the sucker for almost an hour."

They finished their meal and pushed their plates aside. Two small children played in the sand on the beach. A flock of large black birds with wings the size of small kites circled overhead.

"Look at those strange birds," Marissa said, observing the large crook on the end of their beaks.

"Those are frigates. The Shipstern Nature Preserve isn't far from here. That's probably where they're from."

Devon swatted at a mosquito. "I thought we'd spend the next couple of days at DuPlooy's, which is over by San Ignacio."

"Sounds good. I'm ready to get away from the coast and all these mosquitoes. Are the Mayan ruins in San Ignacio?"

"There are ruins throughout the rain forest, but Caracol, south of San Ignacio, is the largest excavated site in Belize. At the DuPlooy's lodge we can arrange for a tour guide."

Marissa leaned forward. "I'm anxious to see them. What are they like?"

"Tall. But one thing I specifically remember from the last time was the ball court."

"Ball court?"

Devon leaned back in his chair. "Yeah, it's a grassy field shaped like a dumbbell with sloping sides. They used a small hard ball and wore some kind of metal thing around their waists that they struck the ball with. The weird thing is that the captain of the winning team was beheaded after the game, so his squirting blood could give sustenance to the sun, and then his spirit could take flight and go off to the highest heavens."

Marissa scrunched up her face. "How bizarre. You'd think it would be the captain of the losers."

"Not a lot of incentive to win, if you ask me." Devon reached over, took her hand, and kissed it. "You look so beautiful. How about a stroll on the beach?"

They kicked off their shoes and made their way across the sand. Devon had his arm around Marissa's shoulder. Once they reached the water's edge, they walked with the warm water lapping at their feet.

Marissa looked up at Devon. "Thanks for bringing me here. These last few days have been wonderful."

Devon squeezed her shoulder. "It's been good to reconnect."

"What happens when we get back to the real world?" Marissa asked.

Devon paused for a moment. He turned and gazed out over the water. "I've been thinking a lot about that. I can understand why you feel uncomfortable staying in the States, so I've decided to put the restaurants and the baroness's house up for sale. That way, we can go wherever you want."

Marissa shrieked with delight, threw her arms around his neck, then jumped up and locked her legs around his waist. She smothered him with kisses.

Devon laughed and walked farther into the surf, holding her close.

It doesn't really matter what I tell her at this point, he thought.

Chapter Twenty-five

Monday morning Shark and Dell took a DMV photo of Hunter Cowan and headed for Savannah.

Once they were at the airport, Dell went downstairs to the courtesy van counter while Shark started interviewing taxi drivers.

An hour and a half later, Shark sat in the lobby sipping coffee when Dell appeared and dropped into the chair next to him. Shark reached down and picked up a clear plastic glass off the floor next to his foot. "How about some decaf iced tea?"

"You are a man after my heart. Thanks," Dell said as she took the glass from his hand.

"Do any good?" Shark asked.

"No. I interviewed all the van companies and only one runs that time of night since there are so few flights coming in. They had one female passenger during the time frame we're looking for, an older woman flying in for a funeral. I need to check the hotel courtesy vans when we get back to the island. A couple of them were here, but not all of them. How about you?"

"I spoke to several taxi drivers. Most weren't on duty then, but I got the names of their dispatchers. I'll call and find out the drivers who were working during those hours. Unfortunately, with the number of cab companies in the city, that could take days."

Dell took a swig of her tea. "So if he didn't use a courtesy van or a taxi, how else could he have gotten back to the island?"

"Call a friend to come and pick him up?"

"I've requested his phone records. If he used his cell, I'll be able to find that out, but if he used a pay phone we could be out of luck. Any other way you can think of?"

Shark pondered for a moment. "I doubt he would be dumb enough to rent a car or hire a limo, but we need to check."

Dell sat up straighter in her chair. "Were there any cars reported stolen from the airport lot that night?"

Shark nodded his head. "Good thought. We need to follow up on that. Anything else?"

Dell closed her eyes and scrunched up her face, a sure sign she was thinking hard. "If he happened to stumble across someone he knew, they might have given him a ride back to the island. But I would think that time of night it would be highly unlikely."

"Let's hope not. That would be tough to follow up on. We also need to trace his movements earlier in the evening."

Dell nodded. "I was surprised when you didn't ask him for more details about his whereabouts when we talked to him yesterday."

"Oh, we're not done talking to Mr. Cowan. We've just started. I wanted him to think about it overnight and stew a little."

Dell took the lid off her glass and began to chew on an ice cube. "He doesn't seem like the kind of person to sit home on a Friday night alone. But since he's engaged, maybe he was there all evening waiting for his sweetie to call."

Shark stretched his legs out straight, crossed his arms, and leaned back in the chair. "Am I the only one that has trouble picturing those two together?"

Dell glanced over at him. "I think maybe you just don't want to think of them as a pair. Even though you protest, I think you're attracted to her."

Shark sat up straight. "You're nuts."

Dell played with her ear lobe.

Shark stood up abruptly. "Are you ready to go?"

"Sure, as long as we can stop and get something to eat on the way back to the island."

"If you're not careful that kid's gonna weigh ten pounds when he's born. Don't you think it's about time to tell the sheriff and go on desk duty?"

"Not until I start showing. Why? You got another partner picked out you want to work with?"

"No, and with my luck lately, the sheriff will probably assign me some rookie straight out of the academy."

Stephanie dragged her weary body into the apartment and headed straight to the kitchen. They'd had auditors in for the past week, and she'd been averaging three to four hours overtime each day. Twelve-hour days were a lot harder than her regular eight-hour shift. She pulled an iron skillet out of the cabinet, opened the refrigerator, and took out two eggs. She didn't have to be quiet. She knew this was the day for Andrea's treatment.

Stephanie had finished eating and was washing her dishes when the front door opened. Andrea entered and threw her keys and several tapes to transcribe on the table in the foyer.

Surprised that she would be finished with her chemo so early, Stephanie asked, "What are you doing here? Your treatment over so soon?"

Andrea sat down at the kitchen table. "I didn't have a treatment today."

Stephanie dried her hands on the dishtowel. "Was it rescheduled or something? I'm sorry I've been so tied up at work that I've hardly had a chance to talk the last few days. Seems like I've barely seen you."

"That's okay. I know you've been snowed under. But we do need to talk."

Stephanie sat down. "What's the matter?"

"I had an appointment with Dr. Bartholomeu a few days ago."

Stephanie slapped her forehead. "I'm so sorry. I forgot all about it. How did it go?"

Andrea hesitated for a moment. "Good and bad. The good news is I don't have to have any more treatments."

Stephanie jumped out of her chair. "That's wonderful! So it worked this time. I'm so happy." She leaned over and hugged Andrea.

"Wait, there's more." Andrea squirmed out of Stephanie's embrace.

Stephanie noticed the wrinkled brow on Andrea's face and knew she was about to hear bad news. She sat back down. "What is it?"

Andrea cleared her throat. "The reason I don't have to have any more treatments is because they're not working. The hormone level in my blood has not gone down at all. So Dr. Bartholomeu felt there was no reason to continue."

Stephanie reached across the table and grabbed Andrea's hand. "I'm so sorry. I thought it was going to do the trick this time. So what's the next step? Is the doctor going to refer you to some specialist or clinic?"

"No. He wanted to, but I told him I was done. Done with all the poking and prodding, done with all the nasty treatments and their side effects, done with it all."

Stephanie began to cry. "Andrea, you can't give up. You have to keep on fighting."

Andrea shook her head. "No, I don't have to do anything, except enjoy the time I have left."

Stephanie closed her eyes. "And how long is that?"

"He doesn't know. He said he's never seen a case like mine."

Stephanie hung her head. "You can't do this to me. It's not fair. You have to keep on fighting. I don't think I can stand losing you."

Tears slipped down Andrea's cheeks. "I don't have the strength to fight any longer. I'm so exhausted at times I can hardly get out of bed, and occasionally I can't say the words I'm thinking. I'm tired, Steph, so tired."

"There has to be something we can do. What about going to Mexico or Europe to see if they have some drugs that aren't available in the United States that might help?"

Andrea shook her head. "No, the fight is over, and I've lost. We have to accept that."

Stephanie leapt out of her chair, pulled Andrea out of hers, and held her by the shoulders. "Listen to me. I will not accept this, and it's not fair for you to stop fighting. I want you to call the doctor back and tell him you've changed your mind about a referral. I'll go with you wherever they want to send you. I promise you will not be alone. I won't leave your side. Now pick up the phone and call him."

Andrea closed her eyes. "No, I can't do that. Instead, let's just spend the time I have left doing things together. Maybe go on a trip or something. Drink margaritas till dawn and eat all the chocolate we want. Just have fun. What do you think?"

Stephanie searched Andrea's face. "Is that what you want?" she whispered.

Andrea nodded her head. "Yes."

"I don't like it, but you're the only one who can decide when enough is enough. I guess we need to figure out how to finance this vacation."

"I'm not real concerned about that. I have credit cards, and it's not like I have to worry about living long enough to pay them off or file bankruptcy. So see, there's a plus."

Stephanie grabbed a handful of tissues out of the box on top of the refrigerator and handed some to Andrea. "Okay then, where are we going?"

"I don't know yet. I thought it would be fun to plan it together. Any place you've always wanted to visit?"

"What's the limit on your credit card?"

Chapter Twenty-six

The van Devon had hired deposited them at DuPlooy's Jungle Lodge, on the Macal River, late in the afternoon. As he stepped out of the van he said, "The last time I stayed here I was in one of the cabins. But this time, I rented La Casita for us. I think you'll like it."

They checked in, and Devon escorted Marissa down the path to their cottage. As they approached their unit, she was amazed to see huge frogs, almost as large as stepping stones, that didn't even bother to move out of the way. They just looked at her as she stepped around them.

Their two-story house with wraparound porches was nestled in the jungle. It reminded Marissa of a large tree house. She took a tour and found two queen-sized beds and a large futon downstairs. Upstairs there was a king-sized bed, whirlpool, and fantastic views of the jungle from the porch. It was as if they were sitting in the trees. She loved it.

"What do you do for meals around here?" Marissa asked as she began to unpack. "I didn't see any restaurants."

"Meals are all family-style, but let me give you a tip. Don't ask for milk. The last time I was here I wanted some for my cereal, and they brought this unpasteurized warm stuff straight from the cow."

"Gross!"

"Otherwise, the food was fine. We have the option to go

171

to the dining room or have our meals served out here on the porch."

"Having them here would be wonderful."

Marissa stepped onto the balcony and looked around. She couldn't see any of the other cottages. It was as if Tarzan had carved them a home in the sky. She reached out and touched a leaf, then looked up to see multi-colored birds singing their repertoires high in the trees. It was shady, the sun blocked by the intertwining limbs. It was difficult to see where one tree ended and another began. Bright colored flowers hung down like clusters of grapes from the branches.

Devon stepped up beside her and handed her a glass of white wine.

Marissa smiled. "I think this is one of the neatest places I've ever been. You feel like you're actually in the jungle."

Devon laughed. "You are."

"It makes me want to set up an easel and capture the vivid colors and images."

"I think you'll just have to take pictures and transfer them to canvas when we get back to civilization."

Marissa frowned. "I'm already out of film."

"I found a couple of those throw-away cameras in my bag, but I'm not sure how many pictures are left on them. Must be from my last ski trip. Later, when we go down to the Hangover deck and bar, we'll get some more film."

"Look! It's a toucan," Marissa said, pointing to the color-ful bird that was eating some kind of fruit.

"You'll see lots of birds and wildlife here you've never seen before."

Devon raised his finger to his lips and motioned for her to be still. "Hear that noise in the background? That sounds like a howler monkey."

Marissa turned to him and whispered, "Will we get to see any up close and personal?"

"You'll see them up in the trees at the ruins. But you can't really get close to them."

"This is absolutely amazing," Marissa said softly.

"We'll need to turn in early tonight. We have a long day ahead of us tomorrow."

"How long will it take to get to Caracol?"

"Around three hours. By the time we explore the ruins and then drive back, you'll be dragging. Make sure you wear comfortable shoes and take a jacket."

As they sipped their wine, Marissa admired the red blooms on the bottlebrush trees and the variety of colors of impatiens that seemed to grow wild.

Devon leaned over and kissed Marissa on the nape of her neck. "How about we try out that whirlpool?"

Marissa turned around and smiled. "Are you trying to get me out of my clothes?"

Devon laughed. "Guilty as charged," he said as he cupped her face in his hands and kissed her.

Two hours later, they ambled down to the building where they'd checked in to arrange for a guide the next day, a picnic lunch to take with them, and dinner to be served on their porch.

Devon took her by the hand and led her down a narrow path to a thatch-covered structure where he rented two horses.

Devon was getting impatient. He thought he'd be back in San Francisco taking care of his little empire and in Sabrina Duval's bed by now. He'd tried to call her several times but was always told she wasn't there, or couldn't take his call at the moment. He knew she was toying with him.

He was ready to get this business of Marissa over with. But every time he started to make a move, someone appeared unexpectedly on the scene, or Marissa appeared on guard. If an opportunity didn't present itself in the next few hours, he'd have to make the long trip to the ruins tomorrow. Not something he was looking forward to. As a precaution, when he'd made arrangements for a driver, he'd insisted that no one besides their guide accompany them.

Marissa was excited. She hadn't been riding since Eric died. Then the thought of his equestrian mishap flashed briefly through her mind. She wasn't sure how Devon had managed to make it look like an accident. But she pushed the thought away since everything had been going so well between them.

They followed a winding path along the Macal River. "You sit that horse pretty well," Devon said.

"I didn't realize how much I missed riding."

"Eric must have been a good teacher. Was he a good lover too?"

Marissa looked over at him. "I don't want to talk about Eric."

"Aren't you even a little bit curious how I did it?"

Marissa shook her head. "No. I don't want to know. I thought we were never supposed to talk about business once it was over."

"Well excuse me. I just thought you might like to know the details." *Be careful. Don't slip up now,* he thought. "You mentioned a few days ago you'd like to spend some time in Greece. Why?"

Marissa's horse plodded slowly along the familiar path. "Because in high school I became fascinated with the Parthenon and the Acropolis. I always wanted to see them."

"So why didn't you go last year, instead of holing up in France?"

"It's not much fun to travel alone. I wanted someone to share the experience with."

"I've never been there either, so it might be interesting to explore the area."

Marissa's face lit up. "How soon before you'll be able to break free?"

Devon paused for a moment. "I should be able to tie things up in about a week or ten days."

"Wonderful!"

"Come here, I want to show you something."

As Marissa maneuvered closer to Devon, another couple on horseback came down the path.

Hiding his frustration, Devon pointed to his right. "Look over there at the beautiful flower growing in the branches of that tree. Tomorrow you'll see orchids growing wild in the jungle."

"I can't wait."

* * *

Late that night, Marissa awoke to find the bed next to her empty. She glanced at the clock on the nightstand and saw it was almost 2 A.M. She yawned. They'd had a wonderful dinner on the porch, relaxed in the Jacuzzi, and killed a bottle of champagne.

Marissa thought she heard Devon talking to someone. She swung her legs over the side of the bed and grabbed her gown off the floor. Moonlight streamed into the bedroom, so there was no need to turn on a light.

Hearing him speaking softly out on the porch, she crept silently in that direction.

"I can't believe Mallory's is going up for sale. That's the hottest club in town. Most nights people line up for blocks trying to get in. It would sure be a nice little jewel in my crown if I could get it before anyone else finds out it's going on the market. Go ahead and put an offer on it first thing in the morning before someone else grabs it. Whatever you think it'll take to get the job done. I'll call you tomorrow night and see if they've accepted the offer or if we need to increase it. Also, I've tried to call Sabrina several times a day but haven't reached her. Send her a hundred red roses tomorrow. Have them put something on the card like, 'I'll be back before the petals fall.' You're good at stuff like that. Make something up for me."

Devon listened for a moment.

"Yeah, I'll be back in a couple of days. I'll definitely be finishing my business here tomorrow. It's taken longer than I expected, but it couldn't be helped. Did you get a new head chef hired for Barron's?"

Marissa stood motionless, then silently returned to bed.

A few minutes later Devon crept into the room and climbed in next to her. A short time later, he was snoring.

Marissa lay awake, replaying the conversation she'd heard on the porch. Everything he had told her about starting a new life together had been a lie. She'd been so stupid. He'd planned to kill her from the beginning. So she had, in fact, been the target in Paris. Had Devon been the one staring down the gunsight at her? Had he smiled as he pulled the trigger, sure she was out of his life forever? Was he also the one who'd followed her in Beaufort? Had he tried to kill her there?

She had to get away from him. But how? If she went to the lodge and told them she was being kept against her will, she doubted they would believe her. She had no money, and Devon had taken her passport. Was she going to be forced to play out whatever scenario he had in mind? Was it going to take place tomorrow? Should she fake an illness in the morning? But that would only delay the showdown. She doubted Devon would make a move as long as there were other people around. Surely, they wouldn't be the only tourists on the trip to the ruins tomorrow. She'd seen several guests in the lodge and the bar. Their guide would be there too. She would have to make sure Devon didn't separate her from the pack. She had a feeling everything was going to be over, one way or the other, in the next few hours.

Chapter Twenty-seven

"Hunter Cowan didn't call anyone on his cell phone after 8 P.M. on the night in question," Dell said.

"And the courtesy vans have no record of anyone by that name," Shark chimed in.

Dell picked up her diet soda. "I flashed his photo around to the drivers, and no one seemed to recognize him. How far along are you on the cab companies?"

"About halfway through the list of the ones in Savannah. I haven't checked the ones here on the island yet."

Dell took a sip of her soda. "I doubt he'd call one from here to go all the way to Savannah to pick him up."

Shark leaned back in his chair and propped his feet up on the desk. "That's why I'm leaving those until last."

"What about friends and business partners? Are we going to try to talk to them?"

"If we don't get anywhere with the other calls, I think we have to. The problem's going to be getting a list. If we ask Cowan for it, and he did call someone for a ride, he could just leave their name off."

Dell stood up and stretched her back. "Maybe we could ask Rebecca Sands for a list of his friends."

Shark rolled his eyes. "I'll let you ask her."

"So if Hunter's our man, why do you think he would have been in the area that time of morning? The only thing I can think of is that if he'd called Sands, and she failed to return

177

his call, maybe he was checking on her or something. Making sure she wasn't entertaining someone else. What do you think?"

Shark paused for a moment. "Or he was drinking heavily and decided he wanted a little nookie and headed to her place."

"Is that the only thing you guys ever think about?"

Shark smiled. "Well, not the only thing, but it's high on the list."

"So when do you plan to talk to Cowan again?"

"I think now's as good a time as any. Want to come?"

"No, you go ahead. I'm going to hassle some people about the trace evidence in the Grimes case. We can't really move forward on that investigation until they find it, and we get a report. Then I'll work on the list of cab companies."

Shark entered the Courtyard Building on the south end of the island and took the elevator to the third floor. He entered Hunter Cowan Realty, Inc. and flashed his badge at the pretty redhead behind the desk. "I need to speak to Mr. Cowan."

"Let me buzz him and tell him you're here."

She spoke softly into the phone then instructed Shark to go down the hall to the first door on the left.

When Shark entered Hunter's office, he found him seated behind a massive desk covered with stacks of papers. Shark decided his own desk was neat compared to Hunter's.

"Have a seat, Detective."

Shark was surprised as he gazed around the room to find no expensive artwork, plaques, or knick-knacks cluttering the room. No pictures of his fiancee or other personal items were in view.

"What can I do for you?" Hunter asked.

"I need a little more information about your activities the evening your car was stolen."

Hunter leaned back in his chair and crossed his legs. "I don't know what else to tell you. I worked until around six or six-thirty. I stopped by Remy's and had a couple of drinks and a bite to eat then went home and waited for Rebecca to call. I was hoping to see her that evening."

"Were you upset when you failed to hear from her?"

Hunter shook his head. "Absolutely not. She's a reporter, and I know her hours are irregular."

Shark leaned forward a little. "I bet that cramps your social life a little. Did you get horny and decide to go for a roll in the hay, or were you checking up on her, afraid maybe there was a new man in her life?"

Hunter glared at Shark, his face suddenly crimson. "How dare you insult Rebecca like that. This interview is over. Get out of here."

Shark stood. He stared down at Hunter. "I know you did it, Cowan, and you're not going to get away with it. You killed a man and didn't even bother to stop and try to help him. Then you drove your car to the airport, made your way back to the island, and reported your car stolen. At the moment, I don't know how you got home, but you didn't sprout wings, so I'll find out eventually. You could save yourself a lot of trouble by confessing. If it was an accident, and you panicked, I can understand that. But unless you come forward now, I'll make sure they throw the book at you. No wedding, no million-dollar income, just a tiny cell for a very long time. Think about it. You've got eight hours to confess, or as soon as I have enough evidence, I'm going to charge in here, bring a couple of photographers with me, and make sure they catch a good picture as I drag you out of here in handcuffs. I'm sure that will make the front page of *The Island Packet.* The choice is yours."

The blood drained from Hunter's face. "Out!" he screamed.

Stephanie and Andrea sat in the living room, travel brochures spread out in front of them.

Andrea stared in disbelief. "We could travel for months and not be able to hit all these places. We don't have that long. How do you want to try and narrow it down?"

Stephanie picked up her margarita. "So is there any one place you've always wanted to go?"

"Hawaii of course, but since we live at the beach, perhaps somewhere more exotic. What about you?"

"This is your trip. We should go some place you've always dreamed of visiting."

Andrea reached for a miniature Milky Way and unwrapped it slowly. "It's so hard to decide. Touring Europe would be cool, but maybe we should do something totally off the wall like take a cruise down the Amazon or something."

"So what's the limit on your credit card?" Stephanie asked.

"Ten thousand dollars."

"That'll go fast. I hate that you have to help pay for me, but I've got only about twenty-five hundred in savings."

"This is going to be my treat for all you've done for me. I don't want you to spend your savings, in case your car breaks down or something. And it may take you awhile to find another roommate, so you've got to be prepared to pay the rent by yourself for a few months. How many days can you get off work?"

"I have five vacation days and four sick days left. So if we do it right and include the weekends before and after, we can be gone about twelve days. I'll need one day to rest before I go back to work."

"If we went to Europe and stayed in YMCAs or youth hostels, we could conserve our funds and buy a rail pass and travel all over."

Stephanie picked up their empty glasses and headed to the kitchen for refills. "Riding the train might help conserve your energy instead of walking all over the place. I bet we could see several countries in that length of time. I kind of like that idea instead of spending all our time in one place."

"Maybe we could hit France, Germany, Italy, London, Spain, and if we're lucky make it to Switzerland."

Stephanie set their refilled glasses down on the coffee table. "A schedule like that would be grueling. Are you sure you're up to it? Maybe we should go someplace where you can just lie around and rest."

Andrea leaned back against the sofa. "I don't have time to

waste resting. There'll be time for that later as I get weaker. I actually feel stronger than I have in awhile. I think it's because I've stopped the chemo. Maybe I'll have even more energy by the time we leave. I say we go for it."

Stephanie hesitated. "What if you get sick while we're gone? It could get difficult being in a foreign country and not being able to speak the language."

"Enough of the what ifs. We could get in an accident on the way to the airport."

Stephanie reached over and squeezed Andrea's shoulder. "Okay, let's go for it. I'll put in a request for the vacation days when I go in tomorrow. Let's try to plan for a month from now. That should give us time to apply for passports and get organized for the trip. What are you going to do about your clients?"

"A couple of places said they would save the tapes until I get back. A few others are going to farm them out to a temp person."

Andrea picked up her glass and clinked it to Stephanie's. "To our trip."

Shark grabbed the mail out of his box and headed inside out of the heat. It had been a long day, and he was relieved to get home. He'd made so many calls to the cab companies he felt as if the phone was still attached to his ear. The only good thing that had happened all day was the evidence from the Art Grimes case had been located and sent to the lab.

He threw the mail onto the table, filled a glass with ice, and poured a good measure of bourbon. He sat down at the kitchen table and thumbed through the stack of junk mail, set aside a couple of bills, and was surprised to see an envelope with Marissa's name on the return address. He turned it over and found printed instructions not to open the letter unless she failed to contact him by a date almost two weeks away. *That's really strange,* he thought. He was tempted, but he tossed it back down on the table instead.

He drained his glass then poured another. He picked up Marissa's letter, carried it into the living room and propped it up on the mantle, and headed to the bedroom to change into something cooler.

A few minutes later, dressed in just a pair of shorts, he sat on the patio and lit a cigarette. He didn't like to smoke in the house with it all closed up. It was different when he could have the doors and windows open.

He thought about Jazz and wondered how things were going with her. It didn't really seem as if she was gone yet, since sometimes he'd go for two or three weeks without seeing her. But he missed talking to her.

Had he been a fool not to go with her? It seemed that women were always slipping through his fingers. First Marissa, then Jazz. What was there about his personality that he couldn't hold on to a woman? Did he expect too much? Had his and Laura's marriage been as good as he remembered? Had he forgotten the times they'd disagreed?

Shark felt he was at a crossroads in his life. Dell too, actually. With Jazz gone and Dell going on maternity leave in a few months, he wondered how he would cope with the two most important women in his life missing. Even though Dell insisted she planned to continue working after the baby was born, he knew Josh was pressuring her to quit. Maybe she should. He'd never want to have to tell Josh or his godson that something had happened to her on the job.

And why had he been so rough on Hunter Cowan today? He knew in his gut that Hunter was guilty, but did he want to put him away because of the crime, or for a more personal reason? What was there about Rebecca Sands that irritated him so?

Chapter Twenty-eight

Marissa was exhausted after a sleepless night, and her mood didn't improve any when she discovered there were just the two of them and Julio, their driver, when they left the lodge a little before eight the next morning. Her fears from the night before enveloped her. She tried to still her nerves. She couldn't let Devon know she was on to him.

Within a few minutes, they were deep in the rain forest. At times the road would be potholed asphalt, other times dirt. Civilization seemed far removed. Occasionally they passed through a small settlement with a few dwellings bunched side by side. Groups of small children played outside their homes.

They'd been on the road a little over an hour when Julio pulled the van into a small clearing. Huge trees that reminded Marissa of the redwoods in California towered over them. They climbed out of the van and moved around one of the largest. The tree's gnarly roots grew out on the surface of the ground. When Marissa stood next to them, they were taller than she was. The bark was smooth and almost the color of bleached driftwood. Birds chattered overhead.

A few minutes later, they returned to the van and got underway again. Marissa knew she needed to keep the conversation flowing as naturally as possible. She asked Julio, "What can you tell me about the Mayan culture?"

"The pyramids were built by farmers and slaves. No animals or wheels. Kings, priests, and warriors live in cities. All others live on farms."

"It's amazing what they managed to build with so few tools," Devon interjected.

For the next hour, Julio continued to pepper their conversation with stories about the Mayans.

"*Senor,* we almost at Mountain Pine Ridge. Want to stop at Rio On Pools?" Julio asked.

"Maybe for just a few minutes, so we can stretch our legs." Devon said.

"What's that?" Marissa asked. *Is he going to make a move there?*

"Patience, my dear. You'll see shortly."

Marissa leaned forward and rested her elbows on the back of the front seat. "Julio, do they know what destroyed the Mayan culture?"

"Not know for sure. Something to do with sun's magnets changing. This cause few babies, and ones that were born not right. Also made no rain and fields dry up. They pray hard to Chaac, rain god, but no help."

"When did that happen?" Marissa asked.

"I think maybe eight hundred AD."

"Tell her about the Mayan calendar and when it ends," Devon said.

Julio steered around a large pothole. "Something bad to happen on December 22, 2012. Big thing. Everything will be all gone."

Marissa was silent for a moment then asked, "Do you believe that?"

Julio squirmed in his seat but kept his eyes on the road. "Maybe. Mayans mucho smart. They know sun to change, and many go inland before it happen. Could be they know when everything to disappear."

Marissa sat back in her seat and glanced at Devon. He grabbed her hand, pulled her close, and whispered in her ear, "What a bunch of hogwash. I don't believe any of it."

Marissa thought about what Julio had said. *Could it possibly be true?* She tried to recall what she'd read about Nostradamus's predictions to see if there was any correlation, but it'd been several years, and she couldn't remember. But she wasn't worried about what was going to happen in 2012—she just wanted to survive the next twenty-four hours.

Devon began to point out different sights in the rain forest in an effort to get her mind off the somber prediction.

They drove through an area of large pine trees and red clay-like soil that reminded Marissa of Georgia. Ten minutes later, Julio pulled into the Rio On Pools parking lot.

Marissa saw a continuous series of pools formed by large granite boulders, many connected by small waterfalls. They explored for a short time, then Devon insisted they resume their journey.

They'd been on the road almost three hours when Marissa saw a sign that said Cristo Ray—population 630. It was the largest town they'd passed through. Many of the houses were two-story and grouped closely together. Her eyes were drawn to one with a police sign out front. It was obvious the officer's family lived on the second floor. There was laundry hanging on a clothesline on the back porch. She noted a rusty yellow school bus parked behind the building. Marissa turned to Devon, "Do you think he drives the bus too?"

"Probably."

"That's the first police station I've seen since we've been here," Marissa said.

Devon nodded his head. "And the last one you'll see for awhile."

About fifteen miles out of town, Marissa gasped when she saw a racing river with a few planks laid across for a makeshift bridge. She couldn't believe they were actually going to drive across it.

"No worry. White elephant here will make it," Julio said as he patted the dashboard of the van. "The water go down. Last week it up to tires."

Marissa's first instinct was to reach for Devon, but instead she grabbed the door handle and closed her eyes.

Chapter Twenty-nine

S hark decided to fix a quick egg sandwich before he tackled the traffic to the island to start flashing Hunter's photo to the cab drivers. Dell was on her way to Savannah to continue canvassing the companies there.

As he ate, he wondered if Brent Grimes would be willing to take a lie detector test. Even though the results couldn't be introduced in court, at least if Brent passed, they could rule him out as a suspect and move on with the investigation. Yeah, but move on where? And if Brent was smart, he wouldn't have any part of it.

Shark was almost finished with his breakfast when the doorbell rang. Surprised that someone would be at his door at seven-thirty in the morning he shoved the last bite of sandwich into his mouth and hurried toward the foyer.

He opened the door and found Rebecca Sands fidgeting on his doorstep.

"What are you doing here?" he asked.

"I've been trying to catch you at the office. But they always tell me you're not there. I've left several messages which you never returned. I need to talk to you. So I looked up your address in the phone book. Can I please come in for a minute? I promise not to take more than five minutes of your time."

Shark could tell she'd been crying. Dressed in a pair of white shorts and a long blue cotton shirt that appeared to have been slept in, her face devoid of makeup, she looked the exact opposite of the put-together reporter he'd dealt with in the past.

"You look like you could use some caffeine." Shark motioned for her to enter.

Rebecca stood in the foyer, her eyes downcast. "Thanks."

Shark led her to the kitchen, grabbed a mug out of the cabinet, and filled it with coffee. "Do you take anything in it?"

"One packet of sweetener and some cream, if you have it."

"I don't have any of that artificial junk. You'll have to make do with sugar, and there's milk in the fridge."

Rebecca opened the refrigerator and pulled out the carton of milk, checking the expiration date.

Shark set the mug on the table, along with the sugar bowl and a spoon. "Have a seat."

Rebecca poured a little milk into her cup and returned the carton to the refrigerator before she sat down.

Shark pushed his paper plate aside, picked up his coffee, and leaned his elbows on the table. "So what are you doing here?"

"I want to talk to you about Hunter."

"You know I can't discuss an ongoing investigation."

Rebecca ran her hand through her hair. "But you can't possibly think he's capable of running someone down and not even stopping."

"That's where we differ. There's no doubt in my mind he did it. Granted, it may have been an accident, but when he failed to stop, then reported his car stolen to cover his tracks, it became a crime."

"I don't believe it, and you have no evidence that his car wasn't stolen."

Shark played with the plastic Tupperware saltshaker. "Not yet, but I will soon. He had to get back to the island somehow after he ditched his car at the airport. It's just a matter of time. I'll find out how. You didn't run over and pick him up did you?"

Rebecca sat back as if she'd been slapped. "Of course not."

"Well, he got back somehow. What about business partners or friends? Would you be willing to give me a list of them?"

Rebecca shook her head. "He doesn't have any partners. And I won't help you hang him out to dry."

"You're just afraid if I arrest him, this perfect married life you've envisioned is all going to come crumbling down."

Rebecca's eyes blazed with anger. "My personal life has nothing to do with this. Are you picking on Hunter because I wouldn't tell you who leaked the info about the lost evidence in the Grimes case?"

Shark picked up his coffee mug and took a sip. "You don't know me very well if you think that."

Rebecca stood up. "Oh, I know your kind. You can't stand to be bested by a woman. And you don't want anyone to be happy, because you're not. I heard your girlfriend ran off to Washington."

Shark's face turned red. "My private life is none of your business. I think it's time for you to go."

"I'll go. But I still think you resent the fact that I won't tell you my source. If that's the case, you should come after me, not Hunter."

After Rebecca left, Shark rinsed out their coffee mugs and placed them in the dish drainer. He wondered how Rebecca had found out about Jazz leaving. Was everyone aware of his inability to keep a woman in his life?

By the end of the day, Shark had interviewed all the night drivers for the cab companies on Hilton Head except for one man, Jamal Harter, who lived in Hardeeville. He was beginning to wonder if he was on the wrong track. He was tired, frustrated, and considering skipping the last interview. But he decided to run by the man's house on his way home, so he could move on to checking out Cowan's friends tomorrow.

Thirty minutes later, Shark pulled into a small development on the southwest side of Hardeeville. The houses were dilapidated. Many had old cars parked in the yards. He pulled up in front of one with peeling white paint and blue shutters.

The windows were open, and Shark could hear a television playing inside when he knocked on the screen door.

An overweight black man dressed in a pair of gray gym shorts and carrying a bottle of beer approached the door.

"What do you want?" he asked.

"Are you Jamal?"

"Yeah. So?"

Shark flashed his badge. "I need to have a word with you."

Jamal started backing away from the door. "Hey man, I didn't do nothing."

Shark slipped his wallet back into his pants pocket. "I'm sure you haven't. I just need to ask if you recognize this man," Shark said as he pulled the picture of Hunter out of his shirt pocket. "Have you given this man a ride in your cab in the last few weeks?"

Jamal opened the door, stepped out on the porch, and looked at the photo. "What'd he do?"

"That's not important."

Jamal looked down at the floor. "No. I don't think so."

Shark wasn't convinced. "I know you took a fare from Hilton Head to the Savannah airport around five A.M. on Saturday morning about a week ago. But you don't show a return fare. If you picked up someone there and didn't run it through the meter, that's not a problem for me. I just need to know if you gave this guy a ride back to the island."

The man looked around and shuffled from one foot to another. "I could get fired if I did something like that. And I really need this job. I was out of work for almost a year before I landed this gig."

Shark's pulse picked up a notch. "Listen, I think this guy ran a man down and killed him. He didn't even stop. So just be straight with me, and I'll do my best to make sure you don't lose your job. This is really important."

Jamal tipped the bottle up and drained it. "Yeah, I picked him up at the airport about six A.M. He flashed a hundred dollar bill and said it was all mine if I didn't run the meter or log the trip on the way back to the island."

"Where did you drop him off?"

"In Sea Pines."

Shark smiled. "Did he say why he didn't want you to run the meter?"

"No, and I didn't ask."

"I need to get your statement on paper. Can I come in for a minute?"

"I'll pull a couple of kitchen chairs out here on the porch. At least there's a little bit of a breeze out here."

Shark nodded. "That'll work."

Shark was excited as he punched in the numbers for Dell's cell phone. As soon as she answered he yelled, "We got him!"

"Whoo-hoo! Tell me about it."

Shark filled her in on his conversation with Jamal. "Meet me at the office, and we'll swear out the warrant. I can't wait to see the look on his face when we put the cuffs on him."

"I'm just leaving Savannah, so you'll get to the office first. Get it in motion, and I'll be there in time to go with you."

Two hours later Shark and Dell pulled into Hunter's driveway.

"Damn, isn't that Rebecca's vehicle?" Dell asked.

"Looks like it," Shark said, unfastening his seat belt.

"This is not going to be easy for her," Dell said as they approached the front door.

Shark stabbed the doorbell. "She might as well learn what kind of guy she's engaged to."

Hunter, dressed in a pair of khakis and white long-sleeved dress shirt, a glass of red wine in his hand, opened the door. The smile on his face disappeared. "Officers."

"Hunter Cowan, you're under arrest for the hit-and-run death of Tomas Sanchez."

Rebecca entered the room, as Shark was Mirandizing Hunter. "Oh my God," she whispered.

Dell caught her eye. "I'm sorry," she mouthed silently.

Rebecca raced to Hunter's side as Shark pulled handcuffs out of his pocket.

"Is that really necessary?" she asked.

"Yes," Shark said as he took the glass of wine from Hunter's hand, turned him around, and snapped the cuffs snuggly around his wrists.

"There has to be some mistake," Rebecca said.

Shark shook his head. "There's no mistake."

Rebecca turned to Hunter. "Tell them they're wrong."

When Hunter didn't respond, Rebecca asked, "What can I do?"

"Call my lawyer, Matt Neely. And don't worry. He'll have me out on bail in a matter of hours."

"Let's go," Shark said as he escorted Hunter toward the door.

Rebecca raced to the window and watched Shark load Hunter into the back of the car. Once they disappeared from sight, she collapsed onto the couch. She couldn't believe Hunter had been arrested. Could he possibly be guilty?

Then she remembered the look on his face: not one of shock and indignation, but more one of resignation.

Silent tears began to flow down her cheeks. She felt as if her whole world was crashing down around her. Her fiancé would be put on trial. If he was found guilty, he'd go to prison. Where would that leave her? She couldn't possibly marry him under the circumstances. On the one hand, she felt selfish for even thinking about herself when Hunter was in such trouble. But on the other, she felt as if a burden had been lifted off her shoulders. And in her heart, she knew she was relieved that she had an out.

Chapter Thirty

D r. Bartholomeu had a cancellation in his schedule. After catching up on his dictation, he stared at the stack of medical journals piled on the corner of his desk. There never seemed to be enough hours in a day to keep up with everything. He was months behind on his reading, and new studies were always being reported, something he couldn't afford to fall behind on.

He sorted through his mail and added the latest copy of *The New England Journal of Medicine* to the stack. He signed several insurance forms and filled out a disability report for one of his patients.

Dr. Bartholomeu glanced down at his watch. Fifteen minutes before his next patient arrived. He pulled the copy of the journal from the top of the stack and began to leaf through it to see if there was anything pertinent to his practice. Half the pages were filled with ads from pharmaceutical companies touting their newest miracle drug.

He quickly scanned an article about the latest protocol for treating the different stages and types of breast cancer then flipped the page. The title of the next article sent a chill down his spine.

Dr. Bartholomeu read the item three times before removing his glasses and laying them aside. He folded his arms and rested his head on the desk. He was overwhelmed with horror at what he'd done, and the thought of the impending lawsuit that he was sure would be filed made him nauseous.

There was a rap on the door. "Doctor, Mrs. Needham is ready in room three."

Dr. Bartholomeu tried to get his emotions under control. He glanced at the clock over the door. Three more hours before he'd be finished seeing patients. He wasn't sure he would make it.

Shark and Dell sat at Applebee's, just down the street from the courthouse in Beaufort, enjoying a late lunch. They'd just come from Hunter Cowan's bond hearing.

"Do you think Rebecca Sands will stick by her man?" Dell asked.

Shark picked up a French fry and dipped it into the mound of ketchup on his plate. "Not if she knows what's good for her. She'd be better off to cut her losses now and head back to Atlanta. It can't be soon enough as far as I'm concerned."

Dell reached for the saltshaker. "Now that Cowan's out on bail and a trial not scheduled for several months, I won't be surprised if he talks her into marrying him right away."

Shark grabbed the shaker and set it outside her reach. "You're supposed to cut down on salt, remember? The doctor said it would help prevent swelling in your feet."

"Yeah, but fries without salt is like coconut cream pie without the coconut."

"What happened to that bottle of stuff you've been carrying around in your purse?"

Dell opened her bag, took out the bottle of Mrs. Dash salt substitute, and sprinkled a generous amount onto her food. "This doesn't taste near as good."

Shark smiled. "Anyway, back to Sands. If she agrees to go ahead and marry him with all this hanging over his head, then she's nuts."

"I feel sorry for her. She quit her job, moved down here to get married, and she goes from planning a wedding to getting frisked when she goes to visit her sweetie. Tough break."

Shark wiped his hands on his napkin. "Enough about Sands. The evidence should finally be back on the Grimes case when we get to the office."

"We're just lucky it was misfiled with a case that went to court this week instead of one a year from now. Care to make a bet on whether it tells us if Brent was at the scene?" Dell asked.

Shark swiped a couple of fries off Dell's plate. "If not, we're screwed. Unless we can get Stephanie to roll over on her brother, which doesn't seem likely. I think old Stephanie knows more than she's telling."

Dell's eyes widened. "Really? I didn't get that impression at all. What makes you say that?"

"Just a gut feeling. Finish your lunch, so we can go see what the lab report says."

Dell wadded up her napkin and dropped it on the table. "I'm done. Let's get on the road."

"Not until you finish your milk."

"We need to talk," Rebecca said as she fiddled with the spoon lying next to her coffee cup. Hunter sat across the kitchen table from her, staring out the window at the high tide pounding the beach below.

"What's there to talk about? I can't discuss the case with you."

"Just tell me if you're guilty," Rebecca whispered.

Hunter took a deep breath and let it out slowly. "Even though I want to answer your question, you know I can't. We're not married yet, and you could be called to testify against me."

Rebecca stared into his eyes. He didn't have to answer. It was written all over his face.

Hunter set his cup down. "Let's get married this weekend. South Carolina doesn't require a blood test, just a twenty-four waiting period after you apply for a license. At least we could have the time together before the trial. If I'm convicted, I'm sure my sentence will be light, since I have no record. Perhaps I won't have to serve any time at all if they rule it was an accident. What do you say?"

Rebecca closed her eyes and shook her head. "I'm sorry, Hunter. I can't do that."

Hunter grabbed her hand. "I love you, Becca. Am I going to lose you because of a stupid accident?"

Rebecca removed her hand and slowly slipped the engagement ring off her finger. "No, not because of the accident. In the back of my mind, I knew it wasn't right. I think that's the reason I haven't looked for a gown or been excited about planning the wedding. It hasn't felt right since I got here. Before, we would see each other every few weeks, and I missed you when you weren't around. But since I've been here, there have been times when I could have come by for dinner or to spend the evening. Instead, I chose to go back to my apartment and be alone. That doesn't sound like someone in love. I'm sorry, Hunter, but I can't do this." She laid the ring on the table.

Hunter stood up, pulled her out of her chair, and wrapped his arms around her. "Don't leave me, Becca. I need you now more than ever. Keep the ring. We can wait until this is all over to get married. Give me a chance to show you how much I love you."

Rebecca stepped back. "It wouldn't be fair to let you think we have a future together. It'll be easier for both of us if it ends now instead of later."

Hunter began to pace. "I don't believe this. First, the arrest, and now our engagement. I thought I could depend on you. Obviously, I was wrong. If you can't support me in the hard times, then you're right. This isn't meant to be."

"I'm really sorry, Hunter. I'll let myself out."

As Rebecca opened the front door, her emotions were all over the place. But her step was a little lighter.

Dr. Bartholomeu hesitated before he rang Andrea's doorbell. He wasn't sure exactly what he was going to say to her. He wiped the sweat from his brow with his handkerchief.

Stephanie answered the door, a package of spaghetti in her hand. "Dr. B. What are you doing here?"

"I need to speak to Andrea. Is she home?"

"Yes, she is. Come on in."

Dr. Bartholomeu followed Stephanie to the kitchen. Andrea was stirring something in a saucepan on the stove.

"Doc said he needs to talk to you about something."

Andrea laid the spoon on the counter and wiped her hands on the dishtowel. "If you're here to try and talk me into a referral, I told you I'm not interested."

"It's not about that. Could you turn the stove off, so we can sit down?"

Stephanie crossed the room. "I'll do that. You two go ahead and have a seat in the living room. Is this personal, or can I join you?"

"That's up to Andrea," Dr. Bartholomeu said.

"Of course you can join us," Andrea said as she led the doctor to the living room.

Once they were seated, Andrea asked. "So what is it?"

Dr. Bartholomeu scooted forward on the couch and cleared his throat. "I'm not sure how to tell you this. I was reading a medical journal this afternoon when I came across an article about elevated levels of the HCG hormone. When you initially saw your gynecologist, he thought you were pregnant. But when the ultrasound showed no fetus, the elevated levels of the hormone were thought to be a result of choriocarcinoma or gestational trophoblastic disease, both rare but extremely invasive forms of cancer that can quickly lead to death if not treated aggressively. So you had a hysterectomy and a round of chemotherapy. Again, your levels remained elevated, and a shadow appeared on your spleen. You underwent another surgery and began another round of chemo. But what I couldn't understand through all this was why we found no cancerous tissue after your surgeries. Well, now I believe I know why. I don't think you ever had cancer."

"What?" Andrea said softly.

Stephanie's mouth formed a perfect O.

"Let me explain. The company that manufactures the lab test most hospitals use to test for HCG levels has discovered problems with their kits. Apparently, they've known about it for a while but didn't tell anyone. They're getting bombarded with lawsuits now that it's coming out."

"You mean I'm not going to die?" Andrea asked.

"I don't think so. And there's a quick, easy way to find out if you really do have elevated levels of the hormone."

Dr. Bartholomeu pulled a Clear Blue Early Pregnancy Test out of his pocket. "I stopped and bought this on the way over. If this test is negative, you do not have cancer. Do you think you can get us a urine specimen?"

Stephanie raced into the kitchen and grabbed a paper cup out of the cabinet then rushed over to Andrea and shoved it in her hand. "Go!"

Five minutes later, Andrea returned to the living room carrying the cup. Dr. Bartholomeu took it from her hand and set it on the paper towel that Stephanie had placed on the glass coffee table. He ripped open the pregnancy test kit and laid it on the table. Using the plastic applicator, he applied a few drops of urine, then looked at his watch to time the test. All three of them hunched over the coffee table waiting.

After two minutes, the test remained negative. "You do not have cancer," Dr. Bartholomeu announced with a broad smile on his face.

Stephanie grabbed Andrea and started screaming. "You're going to be okay. Can you believe it? It's almost like a miracle or something."

Andrea was stunned, her mind a jumble of thoughts.

Dr. Bartholomeu sat down next to Andrea on the couch. "I know this is a shock. I felt the same way when I read the article. I'm so sorry for all you've gone through unnecessarily." His eyes had tears in them, and his voice broke as he said, "I feel terrible that you underwent a hysterectomy and will never be able to have children. I'm so, so sorry."

"Are you sure I'm really okay?" Andrea asked.

"Ninety-nine percent. I want you to come in tomorrow for a blood test, just to be sure. I'll insist the lab use a test kit that the article said has very few false positives. Will you do that?"

"Don't worry, Doc. I'll have her there first thing in the morning," Stephanie said.

Dr. Bartholomeu stood. "I'd better go. We'll talk more in the morning."

"Are you sure you don't want to hang around, Doc? I feel a party coming on," Stephanie said, dancing around the room.

Bartholomeu smiled. "I'll leave that to you two."

As soon as the doctor left, Stephanie picked up the phone, called her employer, and said she was sick and wouldn't be in to work.

Andrea sat quietly on the couch.

"Are you okay?" Stephanie asked. "I can't believe I'm not peeling you off the ceiling."

"I think I'm in shock. Maybe you'd better pinch me, so I'll know this isn't a dream."

Stephanie sat down on the couch. "I can't imagine how you must feel. You had a death sentence hanging over you, and now it's gone."

The color drained from Andrea's face. "I think I'm going to be sick," she said as she jumped off the couch and ran toward the bathroom.

Chapter Thirty-one

As soon as the detectives entered the office, Shark rummaged through the stack of papers on his desk. "Got it," he said as he ripped open a manila envelope.

Dell collapsed into her chair and slipped her shoes off. "So, what's it say?"

"Nothing much. The four cigarette butts had the victim's DNA, and the beer can had his prints on it. The blond hairs we found were human, but there were no roots on them, so they probably came from a wig. Not a damn thing to put Brent there," Shark said as he threw the report on his desk.

"So do you think the shooter was female?"

Shark sat down and leaned back in his chair. "Not necessarily. They could have come from one of old Art's female guests or from a man's toupee."

"So we're back to square one."

Shark nodded. "With as little as we recovered from the crime scene, I'm not surprised. I don't know how we can expect to solve this one with so little evidence unless an eye witness comes forward. Especially after this length of time. I think this one is going to stay in the open case file, even though I'm pretty sure Brent is our man."

"Maybe not," Dell said as she stood up and starting pacing. "Andrea Michaels owns a blond wig."

"Along with about a jillion other women."

"But what if Andrea saw how upset her roommate was

when her father kept trying to contact her? From the number of calls he made to their home and to Stephanie's cell phone, I imagine Stephanie would have been pretty upset. And if Stephanie told Andrea about him showing up at work that day and trying to pull her into his car, maybe she was afraid Art would kidnap Stephanie or harm her."

Shark shook his head. "I don't buy it. The woman is sick, probably dying. And you think she decides to off her roommate's father just because he was calling her all the time?"

Dell massaged her forehead. "Just go with me here for a minute. Consider this. If she knows she's dying, what does she have to lose if she kills him? She'll never live long enough to stand trial. And maybe she figures she owes it to her roommate after all Stephanie's done taking care of her and all."

"So the night before she has a chemotherapy treatment, she just runs out and shoots Art Grimes?" Shark asked.

"We know Stephanie was at work. But we didn't ask Andrea where she was. Maybe we should have."

"I still can't visualize Andrea creeping up and shooting Grimes point blank in the back of the head. But I guess it wouldn't hurt to talk to her again and ask for a couple of hairs from her wig so we can rule her out."

Dell crammed her feet back into her shoes.

The detectives knocked on the door to Stephanie's and Andrea's apartment. They could hear loud music playing.

Stephanie was smiling as if she'd just won the lottery when she answered the door. She took a sip from the cocktail glass in her hand. When she saw Shark and Dell she said, "Sorry, guess we need to turn the music down. Did Mrs. Blankenship call and complain?" she asked as she leaned her head out and looked next door.

Shark shook his head. "No, we need to speak to Andrea. Is she home?"

"Yep. Come on in. We're having a celebration."

As the detectives entered the apartment, they detected a foul odor. "Is something on fire?" Dell asked.

Stephanie looked over at Andrea, who was sitting on the couch, a wastebasket at her feet. They both started giggling.

"Not anymore," Stephanie said as she stepped over to the CD player and turned the volume down. "Have a seat."

Shark noticed that the smile on Andrea's face had been replaced by a frown.

"So what are you celebrating?" Dell asked, noting the blender filled with what appeared to be frozen margaritas resting on the coffee table.

"It's a miracle! Andrea doesn't have cancer after all!" Stephanie blurted out as she plopped down in a chair. Andrea remained silent as Stephanie explained their visit a short time earlier from Dr. Bartholomeu.

"I know it may be a little premature," Stephanie said, glancing over at the silk scarf covering Andrea's head. "But we just couldn't resist burning her wig since she's not going to need it any longer. That's what you smell," Stephanie said with a flourish. "Can you believe it?"

"That's an amazing story," Shark said. "Sort of like being on death row and having your sentence commuted." He observed Andrea closely. Her face suddenly lost all its color, and her hand began to tremble as she set her glass on the table. Her pupils were the size of dimes when she looked at him.

"I'd say that's a pretty good analogy," Stephanie said. "You said you were here to talk to Andrea. What about?"

Shark leaned forward on the couch. "We finally received a report today on the evidence from your father's crime scene. It had been misplaced. The hairs we recovered turned out to be from a blond wig. Seeing as how your roomie here had one on when we saw you recently, we thought we'd just take a few strands, so we could rule her out as a suspect."

Stephanie chuckled. "You suspect Andrea? Give me a break. Is that the best you can come up with? Just because she grew up on a farm and used to go rabbit hunting with her dad doesn't mean she's capable of shooting my father."

Stephanie was surprised that Andrea remained mute. She

glanced over, and they locked eyes. There was a palpable tension in the room.

Then Stephanie looked Shark in the eye and said confidently, "Well, I'm sorry you didn't get here just a little earlier, because I'm sure the hairs in Andrea's wig would not have matched those you recovered. Andrea was in bed when I left for work that night. She'd taken a sleeping pill to help her rest since she knew her chemotherapy appointment was the following morning. Knowing my dad's history, he could have had a dozen women in and out of his house. So I guess you'll have to look elsewhere for your suspect."

Dell glanced at Andrea. Her initial euphoria had evaporated, and she sat hunched on the couch, as if she was a turtle trying to draw its head into its shell to escape from the world. And in that instant Dell knew she'd been right—that Andrea had killed Art Grimes.

"Do you own a gun, Andrea?" Dell asked.

"No, she doesn't," Stephanie answered.

"Why don't you let Andrea speak for herself?" Shark said.

Andrea looked at him. "No, I don't."

"So would you be willing to let us search the premises?" Dell asked.

"Not without a warrant," Stephanie said.

"Stephanie, just stop it. Of course they can search the apartment. I don't have anything to hide. I was not involved."

"Excuse me," Dell said as she stood and hurried down the hall.

"Is there anything you'd like to tell me, Andrea?" Shark asked.

He noticed Andrea's sudden change in demeanor. She sat up straight and seemed to grow a spine. She looked him in the eye and spoke in a calm voice. "No, detective, I have no information that will help you solve your case. I'm shocked you believe I could be involved. The only thing I've been focused on was how to get through my treatments and survive another day. How can you think I'd be capable of murdering someone when I know how precious life is? I'm appalled you'd consider me capable of such a terrible thing. So do your search or whatever you need to do to get me off your suspect list."

Dell reentered the room and shook her head.

Shark realized he was not going to get a confession. He stood. "I guess that's all for now. I'll let you two get back to your celebration."

Stephanie escorted them to the door and closed it tightly behind them. She leaned on the door for a minute, gathering her thoughts before she returned to the living room.

"So let's get this party back in gear," she said as she turned the music back up, although not as loud this time. "I'm ready for another margarita, how about you?"

"Stephanie," Andrea said softly.

"That sounds like a yes to me."

Shark started the car. "Well, you hit that nail on the head. Looks like old Andrea was the shooter. Sure fooled me."

"Me too, but I doubt we'll ever be able to prove it. Especially with the wig gone. Do you think Stephanie was involved too?"

Shark shook his head. "Not really. But I think she put the pieces together as we talked. Maybe we should consider a search warrant and see if we can recover some hair from Andrea's comb and brush or from her clothes. We might be able to come up with a few strands."

"Yeah, I guess we could think about that," Dell said as she played with the little ball of hair in her pants pocket that she'd removed from the comb and brush in Andrea's bathroom. "I checked them out when I was in her room, but I didn't find anything. Sure would like to be a fly on the wall about now in their apartment. I bet they're talking about it."

Shark shook his head. "Maybe, but I don't think so. I'm not sure Stephanie wants to know for sure. That way she doesn't have to face what her roommate did for her. She can just keep telling herself some anonymous person is responsible. That way she bears no guilt."

"You could be right. Do you think if we took Andrea in for questioning, she'd crack?"

"Five minutes after we got there, I would have said yes, but now I'd say no. It was like she suddenly got herself under control. I think she realized that if she didn't, the whole rosy future she was contemplating again would go up in smoke just like her wig."

"If only we'd gotten there just a little earlier," Dell said.

"If only they hadn't misfiled the evidence, we would have had plenty of time."

"So where do we go from here?" Dell asked.

Shark thought for a moment before he answered. "We have no evidence, we can't place her at the crime scene, and she doesn't have much of a motive. I think although one death sentence has been lifted from Andrea, she's sentenced herself to another one. One she will have to live with for the rest of her life. And that won't be easy for her. Personally, I believe we've spent enough time on this case. Time to move on. What's your opinion?"

Dell smiled. "I agree."

Shark dropped Dell off at home and decided to stop at Banana's for a drink. When he entered the bar, he noticed Rebecca Sands perched on a barstool. The only empty seat was right next to her. He considered turning around and walking out. Instead, he took a deep breath, not sure he was ready to deal with the pesky reporter. Maybe he'd just ignore her. He crossed the room and eased onto the seat next to her.

Rebecca turned to see who had sat down. She rolled her eyes when she saw Shark. "Geez. Can't a girl even get a drink without the cops appearing?"

"I'm surprised to find you in Beaufort," Shark said.

"I was over here covering a school board meeting. Talk about something that will put you to sleep."

Shark chuckled. "So how's your fiancé? Staying out of trouble, I hope."

The bartender approached, and Shark ordered a bourbon and coke and told the man to bring Rebecca a refill.

Rebecca fiddled with her swizzle stick. "I don't know how Hunter's doing. We broke up."

Shark was surprised. "You did?"

"Yeah, I think in my heart I knew the relationship wasn't working. It just took the arrest to open my eyes."

Shark grabbed a handful of peanuts from the basket on the bar. "I think it's a blessing in disguise. No offense, but I could never picture you two together. So I guess you'll be heading back to Atlanta."

Rebecca shook her head. "Not for awhile. I signed a year's contract with the newspaper."

The bartender set two glasses down in front of them.

"I'm sure under the circumstances they wouldn't hold you to it," Shark said as he picked up his drink.

Rebecca drained her glass, pushed it aside, and reached for her refill. "I've had enough changes in my life for the moment. Think I'll stick around for a little while. What about you? Heard from your girlfriend in Washington?"

"Nope. It's probably better that way."

Rebecca turned to Shark and stuck out her hand. "How about a truce? I need a friend down here, and I haven't found one yet."

Shark looked at her hand and paused momentarily before taking it. "But this doesn't mean you're going to get any insider information on my cases."

Rebecca smiled. "Understood."

"So tell me, do you like to fish?"

"I've never been, but I'm willing to learn."

Shark grabbed his glass and saluted her. "That's the right attitude. Now about that insider you got the information from about losing the evidence in the Grimes case."

Rebecca burst out laughing. "Do you really want to know?"

Chapter Thirty-two

Marissa became increasingly nervous the closer they drew to the ruins. She attempted to keep the conversation going so Devon wouldn't notice. "So can we drive over the whole area?" Marissa asked.

Devon started shaking his head. "No. Caracol is spread out over thirty miles. Most of it's still covered by jungle. And anyway, by the time we climb all the stairs to the top of the temple and astronomical observatory, you'll be ready to call it a day."

A few minutes later, they pulled into a clearing. Marissa's heart began to race when she saw no other vans or people in the vicinity. However, as long as Julio was around she didn't think Devon would make a move.

As soon as Julio opened the van door, Marissa could hear the howler monkeys. "You get papers there at the visitor's center to tell about ruins."

Devon slung a pair of binoculars around his neck and put his camera in the small hamper with their picnic lunch. Marissa, mouth gaping, stared at several large temples. She shaded her eyes from the sun and gazed at the architectural wonders that jutted far into the sky.

"I wait here. We need to start back by three o'clock, so we travel in daylight. Also, rattlesnakes come out at night," Julio said.

"Rattlesnakes?" Marissa asked.

"*Si*, they come down out of forest and lie on roads after dark for heat of road, especially in Mountain Pine Forest. Villagers walk roads at night. Many die from snake bites."

"We'll make sure we're back on time," Devon said as he took Marissa's hand and led her in the direction of the visitor's center.

"You're welcome to join us, Julio," Marissa called over her shoulder as Devon escorted her away.

"No. I take siesta while wait for you."

They picked up several pamphlets and wandered around looking at various structures.

Marissa glanced over at the largest temple, Caana. "I can't believe how tall it is."

"According to the pamphlet, it's a hundred and forty-five feet."

"How many steps to the top?"

Devon glanced down at the brochure. "It doesn't say."

"It's amazing to think the Mayans lived here for twenty centuries, then just suddenly disappeared," Marissa said.

"And to build something like the observatory over there."

"Whole families must have worked for years," Marissa said as she took a sip from her bottle of water.

"It's hard to imagine a hundred and eighty thousand people living here," Devon said as he glanced around. "Are you ready to tackle the steps?"

Marissa hesitated. "I don't know. It'd be okay with me if we just wandered around down here."

"Not a chance. You're not going to come all this way and not go to the top. Trust me. You'll be glad you made the climb."

"But I'm already short of breath. This altitude takes some getting adjusted to."

"Come on. Suck it up. You don't have to be a martyr on the way up. Stop and rest when you get tired."

They stumbled upon several iguanas sunning themselves as they crossed the plaza. Marissa snapped a couple of pictures with Devon's camera. Exotic birds flew overhead, and even though she couldn't see the howlers, she could hear them.

"Ready?" Devon asked as they approached the base of the temple.

She handed Devon the camera, then stooped down, and tightened her shoelaces. Now that they were alone and about to climb to the top, Marissa knew this was where it was going to happen and that one of them wouldn't be coming down. She felt her senses heighten. Was she about to die, or would she finally be free of Devon? Would she get an opportunity to put the past behind her and start over? It was reckoning day. She took a deep breath and stood up. "Now I am."

Marissa looked up. "Wow. Those are really big steps, but they're so narrow."

"That's because the kings were tall, whereas the common people were much shorter. You go first so I can watch that cute butt of yours. That'll motivate me to keep moving."

Marissa had gone only about twenty-five steps before she was out of breath and her calves and thighs started burning. The steps were so narrow she couldn't put her whole foot on them, so the muscles in the back of her calves took the brunt of the work. She stopped for a moment, put her hands on her knees, and tried to slow her breathing.

"Take your time. You've got a long way to go."

After a couple of minutes, Marissa began to climb again. She didn't look around, just concentrated on taking the next step. Grass grew in between the cracks. She could hear Devon breathing heavily behind her.

A short time later, her legs began to tremble. Finally, she shrugged out of her jacket and tied it around her waist then collapsed onto the narrow step. "I have to rest for a minute. This is insane. I didn't realize how out of shape I am."

Devon pulled off his windbreaker and tied it around his shoulders then gratefully sat down three steps below her. "Just keep telling yourself what an awesome view there will be at the top."

"If I don't have a heart attack before I get there."

"Well, if it helps any, going down is a lot easier."
Will I be going back down?

Marissa glanced over to where Julio had parked the van. She could see him watching them from the shade of a tree. She rose and continued to climb.

Finally, she struggled up the last step and collapsed onto the flat stone deck. Her lungs were burning, and her heart was beating so hard it felt as if her chest would rip open. Devon sat down next to her. He didn't even try to talk for a couple of minutes.

Devon took a sip of water and handed the bottle to Marissa. "Can you imagine doing that every day and then trying to work once you made that climb? No wonder the kings just stayed up here."

It was a full five minutes before Marissa stood up. She stared in awe. She could see for miles. "We're higher than the trees. You can see out all across the jungle."

"Pretty awesome, isn't it?"

"This really gives you a sense of how large the whole complex was," Marissa said.

Devon grabbed her hand. "Come on, let's walk around and take some pictures."

Marissa's first instinct was to jerk her hand away, but she fought the urge.

They explored the carvings and enjoyed the view for the next forty-five minutes. The flat stone terrace extended around the whole structure, but Marissa stayed well away from the edge since there was no railing. On one side, there was a stone platform built out as an extension. "That must be where they sacrificed people," Marissa said.

"It is. I've got only a couple of shots left on this roll of film. Stand over there by it, and I'll take your picture."

Marissa froze. All her instincts were screaming for her to run away.

"I don't feel like doing it right now, maybe later. I'm famished. Why don't we eat lunch first?"

"Oh, go on. Stand over there where I told you, so I can finish this. I can see we're going to have to spend some time reeducating you since you seem to have forgotten who the master is."

Two words echoed in Marissa's head. *Finish this. Is he going to throw me over the side, and make it look like an accident? Who would question it? No one. Is that why he brought me here? Has the time come?*

Marissa met his gaze and wrenched her arm free. "I'm tired of you ordering me around. I need something to eat and drink. I'm starting to feel dizzy."

Devon glared at her then began to smile. "Okay, we'll have lunch first. There's some shade over there."

As Devon opened the picnic hamper and began to lay out their lunch, Marissa took a deep breath and said, "I've made a decision. I'm going to return to France. I can see this isn't going to work out between us. Just give me my cut, and you'll never hear from me again."

Devon chuckled as he handed her an egg salad sandwich and a bag of potato chips. He placed the brownies on top of the hamper. He unwrapped his sandwich and took a bite before bothering to reply. "How many times do I have to say it? You're not going anywhere. Do you honestly think I would let the only person who can put me in jail just turn around and walk away?"

"But I couldn't turn you in without landing myself in prison at the same time."

"Actually, you might be able to if you made a deal. But it doesn't matter. You're not going anywhere. And you aren't very smart to bring it up."

Marissa could hardly choke down the food in her mouth.

Devon finished his second sandwich, wiped his hands on his pants, and stood up. "I've got to pee. I'll be right back."

As Devon walked a short distance away and relieved himself, Marissa grabbed the aluminum foil that contained the brownies, opened the vial on her bracelet and sprinkled the contents across them, then placed them back on the hamper.

Devon sat back down. "Ready for dessert?"

"You know me. I'm always ready for anything chocolate."

Devon opened the foil and passed it over to Marissa. She

took a brownie and immediately bit into it. "Really good." She was so full of emotion she could barely swallow the small piece in her mouth.

Devon picked up one and wolfed it down in three bites. He was reaching for another when he began to cough a little. Suddenly he started scratching his arms. His face turned red, and his tongue began to swell. He ripped at the collar of his shirt. "I can't breathe," he said clumsily.

Marissa felt like she was having an out-of-body experience, hovering above them, watching as Devon struggled for air.

He began panting, trying to draw more oxygen into his lungs. "I must be allergic to something in the food. Help me!" he implored, reaching across for Marissa's arm. His tongue was so swollen he could hardly speak, and his eyes were mere slits.

Marissa scooted back out of his reach. "I guess you really are allergic to peanuts."

"What did you do?" he slurred.

"I just sprinkled a little peanut oil on the brownies."

"Why?" he whispered.

"Because you would never have let me go. I'd always be looking over my shoulder wondering if I would be the next one to die. I heard you on the phone last night talking about making an offer on another restaurant. What you told me about selling everything and moving to Greece was a lie. And I heard you say you'd be finishing your business today. Am I your business, Devon? Were you planning to throw me over the side while we're up here? You've had lots of practice making murder look like an accident."

Devon lunged at her, knocking her backwards, and wrapped his hands around her neck. Marissa beat at him and tried to remove his vice-like grip. He tried to speak, but only a squeak came out. The face above her was unrecognizable, Devon's tongue so swollen it protruded from his mouth, but the grip around her neck continued to tighten. Marissa couldn't breathe. She began to panic. She bit his ear, but he didn't respond. She pulled out a fistful of his hair. The roar in her ears sounded like a freight train. Darkness began to descend as her brain was starved of oxygen. She knew she was dying. Were they destined to die together?

Just as she felt her lungs were about to burst, the grip around her neck began to loosen slightly. She pulled at Devon's hands frantically. She sucked in precious air and began to cough. His weight kept her from expanding her lungs completely. Devon drew his last breath and gave a long sigh. Marissa began to cry and worked to slide Devon's body off her. She finally extricated herself, stood up, and began screaming.

The sound echoed throughout the jungle.

She was still crying hysterically by the time Julio reached her fifteen minutes later.

Marissa twisted the swizzle stick nervously around in her glass and glanced around the small bar in Belize City, just a few miles from the airport. She'd spread Devon's ashes in the Macal River a few hours earlier then raced to the airport, anxious to get back to civilization. But all the flights had been cancelled due to a strong band of thunderstorms from a tropical storm off shore.

Marissa drained her glass and motioned to the bartender for another. Although she would have preferred to fly straight home to France, she needed to spend a few days in San Francisco. As soon as she arrived, she planned to contact Devon's business partner and find out the name of Devon's attorney. Surely, he'd be able to close down the baroness's house, sell the restaurants, and take care of liquidating Devon's assets.

As the bartender removed Marissa's empty glass and set another margarita in front of her, she asked "How long do these storms usually last?"

"Sometimes for days."

"They cancelled my flight. I have to get out of here."

The bartender chuckled and shook his head. "No way. I'd guess it'll be a couple of days at least."

Marissa ran her hands through her hair and tried to quell

her rising panic. She had to get out of Belize. At any moment, the police could swoop down, arrest her, and throw her behind bars for the rest of her life.

"Look. I have to get to San Francisco immediately. It's a life and death situation. I can pay top dollar. Do you know where I can charter a plane?"

The bartender pointed to a table over in the corner. "That guy over there is the only pilot I know who might be crazy enough to fly in this."

Marissa drew some bills out of her purse, paid for her drink, and included a generous tip. "Thanks. By the way, what's the guy's name?"

"Eddie."

Marissa carried her drink over to Eddie's table, pulled out a chair, and sat down. The man's head rested on his arm, and he snored softly. "Excuse me," she said, poking him on the shoulder. When she got no response, she tried again.

Eddie opened one eye and peered up at her. "Didn't your momma ever tell you it's not polite to interrupt someone's sleep?"

"She always said that as long as you compensate the person handsomely, preferably in cash, most people wouldn't object."

"Cash, ah, the magic word," Eddie said as he stretched then picked up his beer and drained the mug. "And what might one have to do to convince you to part with some of the green stuff?"

Marissa leaned her elbows on the table. "If you're not too drunk, fly me out of here as soon as possible."

"Don't you worry that pretty head of yours. I can fly better after a couple of beers than when I'm sober. Where you wanting to fly off to?"

"If you can get me to Mexico City I can catch a commercial flight on to San Francisco."

"That'll cost you a pretty penny in this weather."

"How much?"

Eddie ran his hand over his heavy beard and said tentatively, "Three grand?"

Marissa stood. "How soon can we leave?"

"Whoa. Let's see the color of your money first."

Marissa counted out some bills and held them in her hand. "Half when we get to the airport, the rest when we land in Mexico City."

"I hope you have an iron stomach. I hate it when people hurl in my plane."

Forty-five minutes into the flight, winds whipped the small Cessna as if it were a paper airplane caught in a whirlwind. Rain pounded the windshield. Marissa cringed at the occasional bolt of lightning she could see off to the left.

A sudden down draft sent them plunging a hundred feet before Eddie got the plane under control.

"Woo-hoo! Are we having fun yet?" Eddie asked.

Marissa closed her eyes, breathing deeply, ordering the contents of her stomach to stay in place.

A shaft of lightning struck the small plane, and one of the engines burst into flames. All the instruments on the control panel stopped functioning.

"What was that?" Marissa asked. "I smell smoke."

"Yeah, but that's only one of our problems. All the instruments are out."

The plane pitched into a steep dive.

Two little girls making mudpies outside their tiny village a few miles from Veracruz looked up at the airplane, nose down, streaming fire.

The girl's mother came rushing out of her hut at the impact and violent explosion. She gathered her daughters close as she stared at the fiery wreckage. She crossed herself. No one could have survived such a crash. Once the fire burned out, she'd see if there was anything to salvage.

Chapter Thirty-three

Four years later

Shark Morgan leaned back in the leather captain's chair and stared up at the seventy-five-foot mast of his Beneteau 57. Hand-built in France, the yacht was one of only a handful owned by Americans. When he'd first taken delivery in Beaufort, writers from sailing magazines around the world had come to salivate over its sleek hull and gleaming mahogany staterooms. Shark had insisted on something fully capable of crossing oceans with ease and comfort.

He sipped an icy Corona and checked his chart. He had just rounded the tip of Hilton Head Island, heading toward Beaufort, and his timing had turned out to be perfect. He'd promised Dell to be back in time for young Josh's fourth birthday.

Shark reached into his pocket and fingered the letter that had changed his life. Creased and dirty from years of handling, he always kept it close, like a talisman of sorts. He'd reread it so often since that day he'd plucked it carelessly off his mantle, he had the lines memorized . . .

Dear Shark,
  If I haven't contacted you by the date on the outside of this envelope, it's because I'm dead.
  My ex-husband, Devon Phillips, has reappeared in

my life. I am leaving to visit him in Belize. I hope every-thing goes well, but he's such a volatile person that I thought I should at least let someone know. I'm proba-bly just being paranoid, but then again, since you're reading this, maybe not.

Enclosed you will find a copy of my will, which I've also forwarded to my solicitor, David Pell, here in Paris. I have enclosed his phone number and suggest you contact him immediately.

You were one of the few people in my life who was kind to me and never expected anything in return. I hope this gift will allow you to buy that boat you've always wanted and to travel around the world.

Always,
Marissa

He smiled, remembering how confused he'd been, how stunned when he'd flipped to the next page and begun to read her will. While Marissa had left most of her assets to charity, he nearly fainted when he saw his name and the number next to it—ten million dollars!

He adjusted the heading as he eased the yacht out into Port Royal Sound and chuckled to himself. He'd been in a complete fog as he dialed Marissa's solicitor that steamy day four years before, speechless as he listened to the lawyer's story. Devon Phillips had suffered a fatal allergic reaction and been cremated in Belize two days later. After spreading his ashes, Marissa had chartered a plane to fly to San Francisco. It had crashed in a storm just after crossing into Mexico. Her body had to be identified by dental records.

He remembered Dell's expression when she'd found him sitting silently at his desk. She'd plucked the letter from his hand and immediately gone berserk, insisting he couldn't take a penny of Marissa's blood money and screaming that she'd known all along the detestable woman had been in league with her so-called ex-husband. He could smile about it now, but he'd had a hell of a time convincing his partner. He'd had to remind her that Marissa and Devon hadn't killed Marcus DeSilva, and it was his estate Shark would be inheriting. He knew Dell hadn't seriously expected him to walk away from ten million dollars . . .

The chirp of his cell phone cut through the soft breeze gliding in off the bow, and he grabbed the unit off the console. "Hello."

"So where's your lazy ass now?" Dell asked.

"I'm just crossing Port Royal Sound. I should be docking in about an hour. Did you call the Downtown Marina and tell them I need a space?"

Dell laughed. "A space? That boat of yours will take up half the damned pier!"

"Hey, don't be calling my baby a *boat*."

"Yeah, yeah, whatever."

"Did my broker send the stock for the kid's college fund?"

"Yes, he did. Josh and I don't know what to say. Thank you seems pretty inadequate." She paused, and Shark could almost feel her trying to get her emotions under control. "Listen, I've got dinner in the oven so don't dilly-dally around out there. Call me when you're a few minutes from the dock."

"You cooked?" Shark wished Dell could see him clutch his heart in a parody of shock he'd often used with her.

"Lots of things have changed since you've been gone, sailor-boy. I'm actually getting pretty good at it."

"I guess I'm gonna have to start believing in miracles. Hey, I need to take a shower and shave so I'll be decent for company. Maybe it'd be better if I just caught up with you at the birthday party tomorrow."

"I don't care if you haven't washed in days and you have chin hair down to your knees. Get your ass in gear, and we'll meet you at the dock. I've got lots to tell you."

"Okay, but don't say I didn't warn you."

Shark hung up, leaned back, and smiled.

He'd enjoyed the past two years at sea. He'd seen sights beyond his wildest imagination and met people from all walks of life. He'd met some attractive women along the way, but hadn't stayed any place long enough to develop a long-term relationship. Maybe he'd have better luck with his feet back on solid ground.

As he entered the Broad River, his mind wandered to

some of his most memorable cases. Some he'd solved, and some he hadn't. A few had been easy, others more bizarre. He was anxious to see Dell. He wasn't sure what he was going to do after getting reacquainted with his godson, but for the past month he'd felt something drawing him back to Beaufort.

When he had the marina in sight, he dialed Dell's number.

"I'm almost at the dock."

"Great. I'll be right there."

"Wait, I've just been reminiscing and wondered what happened to a couple of people."

"Who's that?"

"Stephanie Grimes and Andrea Mitchell."

"Oh, the roommates. I still see them around the island occasionally."

"Did Rebecca Sands go back to Atlanta?"

Dell burst out laughing. "Are you kidding? She's now a senior editor of *The Island Packet*."

"I can't say that surprises me."

"Listen, I'll fill you in on all the dirt in just a few minutes. I'm on my way!"